Lyla Evans

ISBN: 0-6157-3653-X
ISBN-13: 9780615736532

Lyla Evans

Rhea Sanchez

Dedication

To Jaden and James:
For you, I choose to be courageous

chapter

ONE

Lyla

My subconscious told me that I was dreaming again—the same dream I'd been having for many years, since turning eighteen. It starts and stops in different places, but I've dreamt the same dream so many times that it always felt more like reliving a memory than dreaming.

My dreams never revealed how I know the man. Whoever he is to me, he makes me feel safe. It's just too bad that in the dream he is waking me up from dying. Even in my dreams, life won't give me a break.

A piercing noise invaded my head, and my dream dissipated as I realized the noise was coming from my alarm clock. I forced my eyes to look and noticed that it was half an hour past the time I'd set the alarm for. I must've hit the snooze button multiple times while I was dreaming. I told myself that if I didn't get up now, I was going to be very late for my first day at work. I tried to jump out of bed, but my sheets had somehow become tangled around my ankles and I landed facedown on my bedroom floor. *Great way to start the day.*

I showered as fast I could, grateful that I had laid out my clothes and reorganized my purse the night before. Twenty minutes later, I turned off the blow dryer, satisfied that it was the best I could do with my long, lifeless dark brown hair. I rolled the lint remover over my brand new black suit one last time, drank the last few drops of my coffee, checked and rechecked that I didn't have a panty line, and bolted for the door.

I took a deep breath before opening the doors to the building of my first official job. I've had plenty of first days, but this was my first official job as a college graduate. I was a little bit nervous and intimidated. I reached to grab the massive wooden handle to pull the door open, surprised how heavy it was.

"Here, let me get that for you," a male voice with an English accent said from behind me. Before I could answer, his hand grabbed the handle, his finger slightly brushing against my hand. I felt a moment of nervousness just from slightly touching this stranger's skin.

"Thank you." I was finally able to answer as I stepped into the lobby. A gasp escaped my mouth: the lobby was beautiful. There was a grand chandelier in the middle of the large foyer. The stranger stepped around me and we stood face-to-face. He was at least a head taller than me. I looked up to face him, but I couldn't get past his green eyes. This man could have walked off an Abercrombie poster. "Beautiful," I whispered while letting a breath out.

He smiled, but my gut told me that it was a sympathy smile. I could guess he was used to girls gawking at him. "The lobby, I mean…" I pointed past his shoulder.

For a brief moment, he looked annoyed. "Who are you here to see?" he asked me, but I didn't detect an accent this time. He beckoned to a security guard to come forward, which led me to assume that this man worked here.

"Oh, crap, I'm late." I glanced at my watch. "It's my first day working here." Thankful that I had put the badge that was sent to me by mail on the front pocket of my bag, I pulled it out. "See?" I said, showing the stranger my badge. But he didn't bother to look. The security guard, who was a few inches short of seven feet tall and who looked like he could be the brother of Rocky's opponent from Russia, bent his head to inspect my badge.

"Right this way, Ms. Evans. I'll show you to the elevators." I followed the security guard and turned to thank the stranger, but he had already walked the other direction and never looked my way. The elevator door opened, and the security guard reached in to press the button for me. "Please go to the eighth floor and look for Ms. Mendez. She'll take care of your first day paperwork."

"Thank you." I gave him a small smile.

The elevator door closed, and I was staring at my reflection. I hate staring at my reflection, so I looked down at my shoes instead. The elevator was fast. I was just about to tell myself to focus when I heard a ding and the doors opened quietly. I walked out and approached the massive reception desk, which took up most of the room. *I guess they go big in this company.*

A young, stylish woman with blond hair neatly arranged in a perfect bun and stylish eyeglasses greeted me.

"Good Morning, it's my first day. I'm supposed to meet Ms. Mendez."

"Lyla Evans?"

"Yes, that's me," I answered too eagerly.

"Please have a seat. Lupe will be right with you."

After a few minutes, a woman about my age, with dark hair and a warm smile, walked out to greet me. I followed her to her office, and after all the new hire paperwork was signed and collected, she explained the benefits and other job-related perks. I was glad to have health insurance once again. She gave me a big smile, "Lucky you—you get to work for Alex. He's gorgeous, and personally I think he's so much hotter than Riley."

I was unsure how to respond to this. Maybe it was a test. She did work for the HR department after all, and I wasn't sure what she was talking about. However, I was sure I shouldn't refer to my boss as hot, at least not on my first day.

"Wait, Alex as in Alex St. James, son of the founder and president of St. James Corporation? They weren't any pictures or bios on the websites—just names and titles." I recalled Alex's name from the company's website. Mr. St. James had two sons, Alex and Riley, both of whom had some major leadership positions listed under their names. I remembered that Riley's title was vice president and Alex's was chief executive of operations.

"Exactly." Lupe affirmed my very slow thought process with a wink.

She walked me back to the receptionist area and wished me good luck on my first day. I made my way back to the elevator and pressed the top button, twenty-fifth floor. An elderly woman showed me to my office and explained that I was working directly under Alex, but he wasn't in the office yet. She showed me where the supply room was located and told me to set up my office to my liking.

By noon, I had sharpened my pencils, rearranged my Post-its by color and size, made friends with the guys in the IT department, and created my automatic signature in my e-mail: *Lyla Evans, Research Analyst.* I couldn't help smiling as I checked the spelling on my name and new title. I couldn't think of anything else to organize, and my new boss still hadn't shown up yet, so I decided to go to lunch.

I walked out of the building and was pleasantly surprised to see my friend, David. He was sitting on a bench in the front courtyard. He stood up when he saw me and pointed at the paper bag in his hand. I gave him a quick hug and glanced into the bag, which I immediately recognized as being from Tommy's.

"Hi, and yay, I'm starving. Did you get chili fries?" David nodded and I reached for one of the hamburgers and sat next to him with the sodas between us. "You came all the way out here just to bring me lunch?"

"The album I was waiting for finally arrived. The record store is on Beverly Blvd, just a few blocks for Tommy's." The one thing David spends too much money on is his album collection.

"Lucky me, I get a free lunch," I said.

"How is it going so far?"

"Okay, I've only had time to arrange my office," I said with a smile. David caught on quickly.

"Ooh, office," he said teasingly. He took a bite of his hotdog.

"Yeah, matching furniture and everything. I've arrived."

"Good, this album cost me an arm and a leg, so you're buying me dinner tonight."

I frowned. Then, turning my frown into a smile, I said, "I knew this hot dog would cost me." It meant a lot to see David; it made me feel less alone. I think he knew it was something my dad would have done if he were still around.

"Which album came in?" David loved music. Talking about it always made him become so animated, and I always enjoyed watching this side of him. Since he was usually on the quieter side, seeing him use hand gestures and hearing the excitement in his voice was a rare treat. His job was at a small recording studio, and he also played bass in an indie band. I often asked him about music in order to distract myself when I started to think of my dad. I think he recognized my ulterior motives, but he didn't seem to mind...or at least he never indicated that he did.

After lunch, I found a file on my desk with a Post-it note attached: *Please Research.*

Finally, something to do. I was running out of things to organize. I turned on my computer and began researching all the significant information that was stated on the report inside the file. The same woman who had shown me to my office tapped on my door. "Sweetie, it's after five. You should head home."

"Oh." I looked at the clock at the corner of my computer screen. Four hours had passed since I started researching. "Do you know if my supervisor ever came in today? I still haven't met him."

"Who, Alex? Oh, honey, you'll have to get used to it. He usually doesn't come into the office."

"Oh," her statement left me puzzled, particularly since she had said earlier that Alex wasn't in yet. Before I could inquire further, she replied, "Well, good night." She turned and continued down the hall.

My cell phone buzzed to signal that I had received a text. It was from one of my friends, Lance. Blue Fish is packed. Got us a table at Rizzos. *Crap, I'm late for dinner.* I printed my report, placed it in the file folder, and left it on top of my desk. Gathering my things quickly, I headed for the restaurant.

chapter

TWO

Lyla

Rizzos was packed as well. I walked around the restaurant looking for my friends. They were at a table by the window, already eating. I took the only empty seat and grabbed a fork to take the last piece of calamari left on the plate.

"Hi, did you order for me?"

"Yup," Lance answered, stealing the calamari from my fork.

"Hey!"

"It was only one piece...definitely would have left you hanging and unsatisfied."

Beck, our other friend, commented, "Funny, that's what all your ex-girlfriends say."

"Ha ha. Everyone's a comedian. We ordered you your spicy spaghetti." For as long as we have been coming to Rizzos, I've only ordered their spicy spaghetti.

"And David ordered you a side salad," Lance added. I looked over at David.

"What?" David shrugged his shoulders. "You need to eat some vegetables."

"True that." Beck sided with David. "I've been telling you all these years. You need your daily dose." I looked down at his plate. Beck had created what looked like an underwater scene using calamari pieces and mushroom caps, which they must have ordered and consumed before I got to the restaurant. Beck couldn't help himself: he always had to be creating or destroying something with his hands.

"Nice," I said, referring to his latest creation.

"So how was the first day of work?" Lance asked me.

"Good but weird. I didn't meet my boss yet. He didn't even come to work."

"Sweet," Beck replied.

"I hope he's not a jerk who makes you do all the work." Lance was always suspicious of everyone and over-protective of me. Since my dad's death, Lance had taken his over-protectiveness to a new level, but I didn't mind. I knew my dad was resting easier knowing that my three best friends were still in my life. In fact, I couldn't imagine my life without them. *Then again, I couldn't imagine my life without my dad either, yet here I am living my life without my dad or a single relative that I know of.*

I changed the subject, hoping to move the conversation away from me. David sensed my intentions and started talking about the new album he had acquired today. My three friends were all the family I had left. My mom left when I was just a baby. My dad was an only child, and I never met any other relative. Between my dad, David, Lance, and Beck, I was never left wanting.

"Are you gonna eat that?" Lance asked, already helping himself to my spaghetti that I hadn't touched yet.

"I was going to save it for my lunch tomorrow."

"Tomorrow? There are three starving men in front of you right now." Beck quipped, and Lance nodded in agreement.

"How can you be starving when you just inhaled a huge piece of lasagna?" I didn't wait for Beck or Lance to reply. "Fine," I pushed the plate toward the center of the table. In a flash, Beck, David, and Lance all jabbed their forks down on my plate, twirling pasta as quickly as possible. When we were in high school, I would sometimes pretend that Beck, David, and Lance were my brothers and we were at our dinner table eating together as a family.

"Seriously, I think their portions are getting smaller and smaller," Beck announced with his mouth full of pasta.

I squirmed at the sight of his half-chewed food. "Yuck!"

"I'm going to start bringing a scale," Beck added, still chewing his food.

Lance wiped the sauce from the corner of his mouth with his napkin and threw the napkin on his plate. Lance jabbed Beck on the shoulders with his elbow. "We got you something, Lyla. Sort of a congrats for your first official job. Get the bags, Beck."

Beck reached behind his chair and pulled out a large bag, out of which he pulled a brown box. "Here you go."

"Aww, thanks guys. You shouldn't have." I shook the box. The box was about the size of a keyboard. "Keyboard?"

"Not just any keyboard, the best ergonomically built keyboard," Beck said with a proud grin. "Give me a call when you're ready to set it up, and I'll walk you through it."

"Thanks," I replied. I didn't want to tell him that I could probably figure it out on my own. It would break his heart.

"All right, mine is next and it's better than a boring keyboard." Lance shoved the box aside and grabbed the bag, pulling out his gift and handing it to me.

It was an unwrapped frame. I turned it over. "A picture of you?"

"Yeah, in case some jerk at your work tries to hit on you. You can just point to the picture and tell him that you're already taken. Or in case some of your lady coworkers ask if you know a handsome and available young man," Lance winked at me. "Bam! There it is, my picture."

"You're not available," David chimed in.

"You're not handsome," Beck added.

"I get more action than you, Nintendo boy." This was Beck's nickname since our high school days. He was the only kid we knew who was still playing with an original Nintendo Gameboy.

"Sorry, Lance, but I would never do that to Irene." Irene is Lance's on-and off-again girlfriend...apparently currently off.

"What? Didn't you hear? We broke up. I texted you." No one answered. We knew better. Lance and Irene would be together again before the night was over. "You guys are lame." Lance turned to David, "What'd you get Lyla, David?"

"He bought me lunch today," I answered for David.

Lance leaned in, "What, you already scoped out her new work? Any hot secretaries?"

"I don't think they call them secretaries anymore, Lance," David replied.

"Whatever." Lance slumped back in his chair.

As much as I usually like to hear the boys banter, I was getting tired. "I should get home," I announced.

"But it's still early. We need to celebrate your new job!" Lance protested.

"It's the last Monday of the month. Don't you need to do the alcohol inventory?"

"Oh, shit. You're right. Thanks for reminding me. What would I ever do without you?" Lance replied as he pulled out his wallet. We paid for our dinner and headed out of the restaurant. David and Beck walked me to my car. Lance headed to the club he manages in downtown Los Angeles.

chapter

THREE

Lyla

By the end of the week, I had gotten used to getting my directives from Post-its left on files on my desk. On Monday, there was a one-page document on my desk. I looked it over; it looked like an agenda for a meeting. I recognized some of the names from my previous week's research.

The following day, there was a slight tap on my door. I looked up and the stranger who had helped me open the door on my first day walked in and sat on one of the chairs facing my desk. He didn't even wait for me to ask him to come in.

"You actually look busy," the man announced as he straightened his tie.

"Sorry?" I was confused by his statement and a bit irritated with his implication.

"I said you actually look like you're working."

"Excuse me?" I said a little louder, not bothering to hide the agitated tone in my reply.

"Let me start over. My name is Riley; nice to meet you." He extended his hand across the desk.

"Oh." I realized who he was. "Riley St. James, vice president of the company?" I shook his hand.

He smiled in response to the fact that I had finally acknowledged who he was. "What are you working on?"

"I've been getting these assignments on Post-its and I figured they were from Mr. St. James." I held up the Post-its.

"I'm Mr. St. James," he replied in a steady voice.

"I meant the other Mr. St. James. The one I work for...I think." I decided to stop speaking because I realized how stupid I was beginning to sound. Riley was staring at me. It seemed like he was trying to figure me out. Desperate to break the awkward silence, I said the first thing that came to mind: "I actually found something really interesting. It looks like one of the buildings the company is thinking about acquiring has been in the news lately, but—"

He interrupted me, "Shouldn't you be telling this to your boss, the *other* Mr. St. James?"

"Yes, but he isn't here...yet."

He chuckled. "Alex doesn't usually show up on Tuesdays."

"I've heard that, and I've heard that he doesn't show up on Wednesdays, Thursdays, or Fridays either. Sorry—"

He cut me off again. "I know my own brother. But listen, if you can get him to attend the meeting on Thursday, then maybe all your research might actually be put to good use. And maybe we'll let you keep your job too." He smiled, but it was that pity smile again. That pity smile was really beginning to annoy me.

"What? I don't understand. Am I being fired?" He shrugged and stood up from the chair. He paused and stared at me again. Then he walked out of my office. I ran after him and called out, "What am I supposed to do?" He never bothered to look back. *What a smug son of a bitch.*

Pissed off, I walked back into my office, sat down on my chair, then got up and marched right out to the elevator. I pressed the floor for the HR department. At the big reception desk, I asked for Lupe. The receptionist with the blond hair directed me to her office.

I stopped at her doorway and waited for Lupe to look up. "What's up?" she asked. I walked in and sat down on the chair in front of her desk. I recounted what just passed between Riley and me. I asked her what my job description was. She typed a few strokes on her computer, moved the mouse around, and read the same job description that I had seen in the ad that I had applied for.

"I know, but how am I supposed to do that if my boss isn't even here?"

"Alex? I've never heard anyone complain before. Most people like not having a hovering supervisor around. I wouldn't mind that." Lupe added the last line in a whisper.

"Yeah, but did you hear what I just told you? I'll be fired if he doesn't show up. Is that even legal?" Lupe didn't say anything. I sighed. "Where can I find Alex? Can I have a cell number or a home number where I can reach him? He needs to be at a board meeting on Thursday."

"Thursday, huh? He usually doesn't show up on Thursdays."

"Yeah, I got that," I said, rolling my eyes.

"Hmm," Lupe said, tapping one finger on her cheek. "If we had his number, it would be in his personnel file, which is alphabetically filed in the cabinet behind me. Oh and look at that, I need to refill my coffee." Lupe winked and walked out of her office.

Taking the hint, I went to the file cabinet. I wrote down all of Alex's phone numbers as well as his home address.

During dinner with my friends that night, I decided that if I was going to lose my job, I deserved another mojito and definitely an-

14

other order of nachos. "Why don't you just go to his house and deliver the agenda?" David suggested. "I'll go with you if you like."

"That way you get to meet him, and if he turns out to be an asshole then it's not worth losing your job," Lance added.

Beck pushed a manila envelope across the table toward me. "What's this?" I asked.

"I looked up your boss," he replied. Beck was a computer whiz who could find anything on anyone in the cyber world.

"Seriously?"

"Just in case—what if he turned out to be a psycho or a repeat sexual harassment offender."

"Okay, well…what did you find out?"

"He's clean. Not even a speeding ticket. He didn't even go to a traditional high school, just had private tutors."

"Any pictures in here?" I asked as I began to open the envelope.

"No. Strange, right?"

Disappointed, I put the envelope down. "I don't want to think about it until tomorrow. Tonight, I want to enjoy my mojito and nachos." I slapped Lance's hand away to stop him from stealing another chip from my plate.

❦

The next morning, hung over, I got ready for work, repeating my usual morning routine in slow motion. Once I got there, I immediately regretted coming in. Seeing another Post-it made me think of the smug and obnoxious Riley St. James. Nevertheless, I did the research. By ten a.m., I had popped a second Advil to try to stop my headache. I heard Lance's voice in my head, "Maybe Alex is just as arrogant and obnoxious as his brother, and you wouldn't even want this job anymore." I turned off my computer and got into my car and punched in Alex's address on my navigation system.

Alex's modern house was on the edge of the cliff overlooking the PCH, the Pacific Coast Highway. I checked to make sure I had the right house. It was nice, to say the least. In the car, I spent a couple of minutes practicing what I was going to say. Figuring I couldn't delay any longer, I got out of my car. I rang the doorbell. No response. After a few minutes I knocked on the door and still got no response. Finally, I rang the doorbell again, this time keeping my finger on the buzzer a little longer. Frustrated, I rang, rang, and rang, leaving my finger on the doorbell. *I can't believe I'm going to lose my job because some lazy, pampered rich guy who can't even be bothered to show up for work.*

I gave up and leaned on the door, thinking about how much money I had left in my checking account. The sound of the locks opening registered in my mind way too slow, and the door swung open. I lost my balance and fell into someone's arms. No, not just someone, a very ripped "someone" with no shirt on, who was tall, lean, and muscular, not to mention still a bit wet and only wearing a towel. *Yikes, who does that? Who comes to their door only wearing a towel?* I looked up and felt an overwhelming sense of familiarity, like I'd seen this man before, but where? His face wasn't the kind of guy you would forget easily. Was he a model, an actor, the eye candy in a pop music video? Where have I seen him? *Stop it, Lyla, and focus.*

I tried my best to regain my balance and focus as quickly as possible. I was finally able to stand on my own two feet. "Sorry, sorry," I stammered. "I was looking for Mr. Alex St. James." *Whatever you do, don't check him out. Don't you dare look down beyond his face*, I warned myself.

"Why?" He was clearly irritated by my intrusion.

I stammered to introduce myself, "I'm his new research analyst, and I need to give him something."

"You're my new assistant?" Great, my new boss also looks like he just walked off an Abercrombie billboard.

"I'm Lyla," extending my hand. "Your new research analyst." I had hoped that by repeating my title, he would catch on that I wasn't his personal assistant.

He briefly shook my hand. "Right, and why are you at my house?"

"Sorry, Mr. St. James, I didn't mean to bother you but you haven't...I mean, you weren't in the office. So I came to deliver the agenda and to tell you that—" I grabbed the agenda out of my bag and handed it to him. "—you have a board meeting this Thursday... tomorrow."

"Well, thanks, but you could have just sent an e-mail or left it on my desk. I'm in a bit of a hurry. I have somewhere to be." *He cut me off just like his brother and he has somewhere to be. God, these brothers have no manners.*

Annoyed, I asked, "Do you know where your desk is located?"

He was clearly put off by my question. He took a deep breath. It looked like he was trying hard to exercise patience toward me. "Of course I do."

"What floor is it on?

"Top, corner office, lovely view of the—"

"Name five items on your desk." It was my turn to cut him off.

"I'm really in a hurry."

"Name five items, and I'll leave you alone."

"Fine," he took a deep breath. "It looks like that's the only way I can get rid of you. A computer, a keyboard, a pen, a phone, and some papers."

"No, there is nothing on your desk except a copy of this agenda. I've tried e-mailing you, I've tried calling you, and I've left several messages." I continued. "I've worked for you for the last two weeks, but I haven't seen you once. If you don't come to the meeting tomorrow, I'll be fired."

"Okay, I get it." Taking my arm, he led me out. I'll see you Monday at nine a.m."

"You swear?" He paused and gave me a look. "I mean, do you promise, sir?" He didn't reply and continued to walk me out. I had just stepped over the doorway when I realized that he'd said the wrong day. I turned to face him and put my foot in the doorway, praying that he wasn't planning on slamming the door in my face. Thank God, he had quick reflexes. Once he saw my foot, he stopped the door from closing. He face wasn't showing annoyance anymore, but anger. "It's tomorrow at nine a.m. The meeting, it's tomorrow," I blurted out.

"Fine," he said tersely.

I moved my foot and the door closed. I sighed deeply and made my way back to my car, thinking that I would definitely be drinking two mojitos later. I closed my eyes and saw an image of my boss' face: dark hair, chiseled jaw line, and hazel eyes. With a gasp I began to wonder if he could be the same guy in my dreams. *I don't think that's the guy from my dreams. Either that or, clearly, my dreams were so off. That guy was a jerk. There's no way Alex St. James could ever make me feel safe.*

chapter

FOUR

Lyla

There was no sign of Alex the next morning. I paced back and forth in the lobby. I had made friends with Simon, the security guard who had walked me to the elevator on my first day. He saw me pacing and promised to ring my office when he saw Alex, if I would stop loitering in the lobby. I went up to my office, but I couldn't concentrate on my work. *This is ridiculous*, I thought to myself, *that douche bag had no intention of showing up*. I was fooling myself.

I drove as fast as the morning rush hour traffic would allow, switching lanes whenever I saw an opening between cars. I was at his house in half an hour. I rang the doorbell, leaving my finger on the buzzer. I felt bad about being this pushy. *Is this job really worth being this aggressive?* I asked myself as I walked over to his garage. I quickly rationalized my behavior as owing to my fear of losing my job, health benefits, the matching furniture in my office, and the fact that I didn't have someone to take care of me financially anymore.

I had to stand on the edge of a large planter to look into the small windows of Alex's garage door. *My God, this man likes his cars.* I saw at least half a dozen very expensive sports cars and a row of motorcycles neatly parked diagonally. *Who are these people I work for?* None of the parking spots were empty, so I figured he must still be home. I rang the doorbell repeatedly. Finally, the door opened and a middle-aged woman in an apron stood in front of me. She looked a bit annoyed.

"Good morning. I'm looking for Mr. Alex St. James."

"I'm sorry, but Mr. St. James is still sleeping."

"Seriously?" I didn't want to believe the woman.

"May I give him a message for you?" The woman had a thick European accent.

I rushed past her. I looked around the expansive living room. I ran as fast as I could up the see-through staircase, which was built to look like it was suspended in the air. I felt like I was going to fall through the steps, and there was no banister to hold onto. I finally reached the landing and saw several doors on one side of the hall-way. I assumed Alex's room was the only one with double doors. I knocked but didn't hear any sound coming from the room. I heard the woman calling after me and coming up the stairs. I knocked again and announced that I was coming in.

"Mr. St. James, I'm coming in. I apologize for the intrusion." I didn't wait for an answer and opened the door.

Alex was sleeping on an enormous bed. The bed seemed bigger than your usual California King. I cleared my throat, hoping to wake him up as well as to help me focus. I had to push back the scenes from my dreams that were flashing repeatedly in my mind. My gut feeling was telling me that this man was clearly the man in my dreams where I die. I couldn't believe that I was standing in front of the real person, yet I was awake. It was too much of a coincidence, but I told myself to process this information later, because right now I still needed a paycheck and the man was lying on the bed just a few feet away from me with no shirt on. *God, he looks like an Olympic swimmer.*

I could hear the woman yelling at me, so I assumed she had made it to top of the stairs as well. Getting over my nervousness, I walked over to the bed and nudged his elbow, but he didn't move. I shook him a little harder, but he still didn't respond. The woman was now in the room. I slapped his arm. He groaned and turned his head in my direction.

"Holy shit!" With a quick reflex, Alex sat up. "What are you doing in my room?"

The lady stood by the door. "Sorry, Mr. Alex, I tried to stop her."

Rubbing his eyes, he responded to the woman, "It's okay, Flora. You can go for the day."

"But I haven't finished cooking your breakfast yet."

"Don't worry about it," he said to Flora as he looked at me. A flash of guilt hit the pit of my stomach, making me feel uneasy and nervous.

"I'm sorry, but you were supposed to be at the meeting. You promised. You made a promise."

"Are you kidding me? Are you crazy?" Agitated, he ran his fingers through his hair.

"You need to get ready for the meeting." As an afterthought, I added, "Sir. Please."

"Give me a break. I've had a rough night." He did look like he'd gone a few rounds in a boxing match. I took a closer look and noticed a minor cut by his right eyebrow and a light bruise on his cheek.

"I'm not leaving without you." I took a deep breath, which gave me just enough time to think to myself, *what a jerk.* "This is my first job, and I'm not losing it because my boss had a rough night and can't attend a lousy meeting." My voice trailed off at the end.

We both stared at each other trying to figure each other out. At least I was. *Why was this man in my dreams, particularly the dreams where I am clearly dying?*

In a small voice, I finally spoke up, not wanting him to look at me anymore. "There's a recession out there, and it's really hard to find a job."

"I'll make sure you get a good severance package. Now leave."

I didn't respond, but just stood there. With a quick breath, I checked my feelings and continued the debate I'd been having with myself whether it was worth working for an asshole who clearly never had to earn his paycheck. I was just about to leave, but my silence must have made him feel guilty.

"Fine!"

"Fine?"

We exchanged another look. "Oh, got it, that kind of fine." I gave him a smile. He tossed the covers aside and got up from the bed. He was only wearing black boxer briefs, and I was embarrassed that I took note of what kind of underwear he preferred. I quickly turned to face the wall. As I said that I'd wait downstairs, he told me to wait downstairs. Actually, it was more like he hissed at me.

"Okay, but please hurry. We only have thirty minutes—no, twenty minutes left."

"I still need to take a shower."

"No, there's no time," I turned around again, only to realize that he was still only wearing his underwear. I quickly turned to face the door. "No, it's fine. You have the whole, 'I just woke up hung over and I got into a fight in bar last night' look. It's a good look for you, the bad boy..." My voice trailed off at the end. I didn't bother to finish the sentence.

He didn't respond. Feeling silly for what I'd just said, I added, "I'll wait downstairs," and headed for the door.

chapter

FIVE

Alex

I waited until she had walked out of my room. I was surprised that her feelings just stopped. One minute I was sensing her feelings, a mixture of anxiety and puzzlement, and then just like that, they were gone. *What's different about this girl?* I asked myself. I had heard a rumor that Father had handpicked a new employee, but I wasn't interested in knowing any more about that...until this morning. I'd always been able to read other people's feelings, even when they tried to hide them. However, this girl, she just switched off her feelings as easily as flipping off a light switch. It didn't escape me that she was pretty, but she clearly didn't acknowledge her own beauty.

I decided to go to this meeting mainly because I wanted to speak with my father, and the meeting was a good place to find him. I looked at my reflection in the bathroom mirror. The scratches and bruises from last night's patrol were still visible. I had become accustomed to the dark circles under my eyes. *How much longer can I go through this?* Running my hands through my hair, I took a deep breath and exhaled. *I need to catch this guy.*

I brushed my teeth and took a quick shower. I felt a twinge of guilt when I saw her sitting at the bottom of the stairs. She got up when she heard me. There was a look of disappointment on her face as she looked at her watch.

"Are you ready, Mr. St. James?" She asked with a polite smile.

I still can't get a read on her. Maybe there's something off with me.

"My car is just outside. I can drive us to the office." She began walking toward the front door.

I walked the opposite way, toward the kitchen and the door that led to my garage, without looking back. I opened the door and said, "No, I'll drive."

"Fine," she said. I think she was trying to mimic me.

She followed me into the garage. I decided to take the black Maserati since it was still rush hour and drivers tended to make room on the street for that car. I slid into the driver's side and waited for her to get in the passenger side. It'd been so long since I had another person in the car that I forgot to open the door for her. She climbed in. I was glad that she didn't comment on my oversight. We drove in silence. It had also been a long time since a girl didn't try to strike up a conversation with me. I wish I could say it was refreshing, but the silence only made me more anxious about why I wasn't able to read her feelings.

I pulled into the parking space next to my brother's car. I cringed when I saw the sign saying that this spot was reserved for me. She was looking at the sign as well. It was very brief, but I was sure I saw her make a face. I got out of the car with the full intention of opening her door, but she was out of the car before I could walk around to her side.

"Here you go." She shoved a pink file folder in my hands and walked toward the building's entrance. She was walking fast and talking at the same time: "In the file is all the research I've done on each of the properties listed on this agenda." She paused just outside the door to pull out a white piece of paper from her bag and place it on top of the file, which gave me a chance to open the door for her. She gave a polite nod to one of the security guards. We walked over to the elevator and she pushed the button. Once we were inside the elevator, she began summarizing her research. She only stopped when she heard the elevator chime, signaling that we were approaching our floor.

When the elevator door opened, she said, "Thank you for attending your own meeting, Mr. St. James." She walked out of the elevator. Sarcasm, the girl could hide her sarcasm well. As I watched her walk away, I couldn't help but smile. It's been a long time since I smiled at a girl.

I walked into the boardroom, and everyone turned to watch me as I took my seat.

"Why, Alex, I didn't think you got out of bed until sundown." This statement was typical of Riley.

My father didn't give me a chance to reply. "Alex, I'm glad you were able to join us this morning. Can you brief us on what you have found out?"

"You first, Father. Care to explain why I can't read my new assistant?"

"Interesting," my father replied, making a triangle shape with his fingers. He tapped his chin with the tips of his fingers, a habit he usually did when he was thinking.

"I see you have met Miss Lyla Evans," Riley added.

I looked around the room to see if anyone else could give me information about Lyla. The curious and blank stares from the other founders reassured me that none of them knew what my father was up to either.

My father finally spoke. "I had an intuitive feeling that Miss Evans is special. If I'm not mistaken, Miss Evans may be the first person you cannot read."

"Yes. I tried, but I couldn't read her. I knew she was hiding her feelings from me."

Dr. Liam Rogets, one of the founders of our organization, chimed in. "How did you know she was hiding her feelings from you?" He still had a strong English accent even though he moved to America in the seventies.

"I made her wait for me for forty-five minutes while I showered, changed, and surfed the Internet. I couldn't detect any feelings. She was like a blank piece of paper."

"You always did make the ladies wait," Riley said, giving me a pat on the shoulder. I remembered the look on Lyla's face and a wave of guilt washed over me.

My father gave his attention to Riley, "It's time to see which gift she might have." Riley nodded his head.

"So, Alex," my father said, turning to me. I took that as my cue to update the founders.

"We initially thought we were after a group of Pure Evils. Recent intelligence alludes to one major Pure Evil hiring street thugs to take care of his dirty work, the cleanup."

"Great, he outsources. How very efficient of him," Riley interjected.

I continued before he could say anything else. "He pays them with cash after the job has been done. I'm trying to find out how he hires these thugs so we can place a mole. Your girl—"

"Miss Evans," my father corrected me.

"Ms. Evans has figured out that there have been six victims so far."

"I thought there were only four!" Marsha, another founder, cried out. Aunt Marsha was my godmother. I knew that this case pained her. She was particularly passionate about protecting young children.

"We didn't know about the other two, but Ms. Evans found them, and the MO matches the other four sites." I pushed the folder that Lyla had handed me toward my father.

"Keep giving her information," my father ordered me. "Anything else, Alex?"

"Yes. Last night's victim was only four years old." There was a silence in the room.

I heard Aunt Marsha repeat my words, "only four years old."

"Thank you, Alex. It is good to see you attend these meetings. Stop by my office later." That was my cue to leave. Riley was right behind me. He cornered me as soon as we walked out of the boardroom.

"Why didn't you tell me you led a raid last night?"

"I didn't know you were interested," I answered, shrugging my shoulders.

"Where are you going?" He hollered behind me.

"To look for my assistant," I yelled, not bothering to slow down or look back.

I found Lyla in her office. She was packing her personal belongings in a box. I walked in as she placed a plant in the box and said, "Nice fern." She looked up but didn't say anything. "Are you relocating to another office?"

"I'm quitting." She stood up, placing her hands on either side of the box.

"You don't seem like the quitting type," I replied, taking the plant out of the box. "How did you find out about the two other sites?"

"What do you mean?"

"There were six sites listed in your research. We only gave you four."

"I figured the company might be interested in the other two since they fit the same profiles as the first four."

"What profile would that be?"

"Abandoned buildings that have recently been crime scenes. They're cheaper, right, since their value goes down? A bit creepy if you ask me. Was this building a crime scene too?" She was clearly avoiding looking at me.

"Does that bother you?" I tapped a finger on the keyboard sticking out of the box.

"I'm not stealing. It was a present. See?" she said, pointing to another keyboard underneath her computer monitor.

"I wasn't thinking that, but what I was thinking is how quickly do you think you can find out more about these crime scenes?" I took out the keyboard and walked over to her side of the desk. I gently pushed her down into her chair and wheeled her out of my way. I plugged the USB cable into the hard drive and threw the other keyboard into the trash.

"Hey, what a waste! I don't even think that keyboard has been used." She took the keyboard out of the trashcan. Very faintly, I heard her say, "Rich people," as she shook her head.

"Evans, focus. What about these crime scenes?"

"Damn," she mumbled under her breath. "I made a bet with Lupe from HR that you didn't even know my name. Why are you so interested in the crimes?"

"Like you said, if we are going to purchase these properties, these crimes need to be solved."

"That's not what I said. Besides, isn't that a job for the police?"

"Evans, as the chief...director..." *Shit, what is my made-up title these days?*

"You are the chief executive of operations."

"Exactly," I crossed my arms. "As the chief executive of operations, it is my job—no, our job—to recommend which properties to buy. You know, being in operations and all." I cringed.

"Is it?" she asked incredulously.

"Yes, and we can't do our job if we don't have any properties to recommend because the properties are still crime scenes."

"So it's up to you to solve the crimes so we can then buy the building," she asked with a skeptical look on her face. I could tell she wasn't buying the lies I was feeding her. I made a mental note that although I couldn't read her feelings, she wasn't very good at having a poker face—her facial expressions betrayed her.

"Exactly, so start researching or doing whatever it is you do." I powered on her computer. She pulled out a file from her box.

"Here you go. By the way, you're not very good at bullshitting," she said, handing me the file. I took the folder and sat down. "I think it's the same guy using all these abandoned buildings as dumping grounds for his victims. There isn't anything similar in size or age of the buildings except that they have all been abandoned. I did find some things that are similar about the victims though." She paused.

"I'm listening." I put the folder down and began pulling out items from her box.

"That's counterproductive," she pointed at me. "I quit, remember?"

"You should at least give a two-week notice." I continued to pull her personal belongings out of the box.

"Good point," Lyla nodded her head. She opened the file. "These are just my notes on what the victims have in common. Like all the victims are all from low-income families, are most likely recent immigrants, and they are all Catholics who haven't had their first communion yet."

I leaned forward and asked, "How did you come up with that?"

"The oldest victim was eight years old, and in an interview with a news reporter, her mother mentioned that her communion was supposed to be day after she was killed. That got me thinking and I checked. There is a Catholic church within a few miles' radius of each of the abandoned buildings and the victims' residence. I was just about to check to see if the families of the victims were registered at the churches, but..."

"But what?" I placed her stapler at the right side of her desk.

"But it occurred to me that this had nothing to do with my work and..." She moved the stapler inside her drawer.

"And?" I asked, putting some of her pens in a black cylindrical container.

"It was probably a waste of time since these families didn't have any reason to register at their churches."

"Why not?"

"Because these days only people who declare church donation as part of their yearly tax deductions would have a reason to register. Someone who donates his or her last dollar wouldn't bother with weekly tithing envelopes."

"It would be better to just ask the families if they attend a church nearby," I said, then I stood up and turned toward the door.

"Exactly. Where are you going?"

"To ask the families; keep researching and call me when you find anything, anything at all."

"Okay. I've listed all the addresses of the victims in the file along with the addresses of their next of kin."

"Great," I turned to leave.

"Wait, so did someone die *here*? This building isn't built over a cemetery or an Indian burial ground, right? No little girls are going to turn around and say, 'They're back'?" She tried using a creepy little girl voice to say the last two words. I didn't have a clue what she was talking about. "It was a *Poltergeist* reference...you know, the scary movie from the eighties?" I shook my head. "Right. Okay, drive safely." As I walked away I heard her say, "Note to self, don't waste jokes on your boss. It's clearly a lost cause." For the second time that day, I smiled.

chapter

SIX

Lyla

As soon as he left, I immediately regretted quitting. I thought about my work situation. If the company wanted to pay me to research crime scenes, well, I was fine with that. It was breaking my heart to read about all the victims who died in these abandoned buildings. I wanted whoever was murdering these little girls to be caught and locked up forever.

I didn't hear from Alex for a few days, and files stopped appearing on my desk. I kept myself busy. Now that I didn't feel guilty about researching things that might not have anything to do with my job, I had plenty of leads I wanted to continue working on.

On the third day, my phone rang, startling me. It was the first time I'd ever heard it ring, and the ring sounded foreign to me. I picked it up and it was Alex. "Evans, be in front of the building in five minutes."

He hung up before I could ask why. I sighed deeply and turned off my computer. Looking down at my pencil skirt and black heels, I thought, *I hope walking isn't part of the plan.*

Alex pulled up just as I stepped outside. He didn't get out of the car and just leaned over to open the door on my side. Between the looks, the money, the fast cars, and the *I can't be bothered* attitude, he was the epitome of the rich hot guy. *Damn, why does my boss have to be so attractive?*

"Get in."

"Where are we going?" I asked as I climbed into the passenger seat.

"Another crime scene." I detected an apologetic tone in his voice. My gut told me that he somehow felt personally responsible for these crimes. I cringed at the words *crime scene.* "I'm not really dressed to a visit a crime scene. I'm more of a sit behind a desk type of person." I prayed that he would turn the car around.

"I want you to see it firsthand. Maybe you'll catch something that we haven't." He drove faster.

"I don't think you understand. I don't want to go anywhere where people have died." I told myself to breathe.

"You'll be fine, Evans." I realized that he wasn't going to turn back. There was nothing left to do but try not to panic. *I should have quit,* I thought. I hate being near dead bodies. At funerals, I can't even make myself go near the casket.

Alex broke the silence. "Did you manage to find anything new?"

"Yes, but you first," I took another deep breath.

"All right, five out of the six families have moved away. But I did get confirmation that the families attended the churches you listed. The addresses of their nexts of kin came in handy." He must have been driving all over California. The building sites ranged from Fresno to downtown Los Angeles.

"Interesting," I said, my mind already spinning. "I noticed they all lived in apartments. Did you find out if they leased for a year or on a month-to-month basis?"

"What do you mean?"

"If the families are here illegally, then chances are they will move where they can find jobs. If they have papers, then they are more likely to stay in the same place, where their children can continue attending the same school. There's a connection between all the victims and the bad guy, and I just need to figure out if it's through the church or with the family members. Maybe it's the jobs the parents are taking or some kind of governmental service they were receiving."

"You said, *bad guy,* singular. Why do you think it's just one guy?"

Funny, I had never thought about it, I'd just assumed from the beginning that it was one bad guy. "Just a gut feeling, I guess," I said. We drove in silence the rest of the way. Then he pulled into a parking lot that was empty except for three dark unmarked cars. There was a massive building staring at me.

"This is not what I imagined."

"What do you mean?"

"I imagined that the buildings were rundown, with graffiti and broken windows."

"A software company used to own this building. It filed for bankruptcy only last year."

We walked in and a man in a white jumpsuit greeted us. "Mr. St. James, we're almost done processing the scene. It was clean as usual. We found a few hairs, but they could be from the previous tenants."

"Show us to the body."

I couldn't move. My feet wouldn't move. "Evans, let's go. We only have a few minutes before the police get here." I willed myself to follow them.

Once I entered the room, the feeling of despair hit me. I closed my eyes and doubled over, wanting to curl up and weep. I felt tingles running up and down my legs, which were beginning to betray me. I felt a steady pair of hands holding me up. "I need to get out of here," I whispered. I felt so cold, and the hairs on my arms were standing up. I knew if I opened my eyes I would see whoever it was that was making his or her—or its—presence known. Then it occurred to me that wondering who or what it might be would be worse, so I forced myself to open my eyes and saw a movement out of the corner of my eye. I turned my head, but there was no one in the room except for Alex and me. *Oh God, please don't visit me in my sleep.*

"It's okay," I said to myself. "I'm fine." I turned around and looked at the room. It was empty except for the small body lying on the corner. "It's clean."

"Evans, the whole place is clean."

"No, I mean, take a look around. The room—it's immaculate. Not one paper clip or even those tiny little round pieces that fall out of hole punchers."

Alex walked toward the doorway to talk to the person who had greeted us at the door. "Where did you say you found the hair samples?"

"In the hallway."

I felt a cold wind, and the ends of my hair brushed my shoulders. I looked over toward the body of the frail little girl. There she was, huddled in the corner by the body, clearly frightened. "Help me," she whispered. I froze and felt a cold wind pass through me again. No spirit has ever shown itself or spoken to me while I was awake. She looked so scared. I wanted to hold her; I took several steps toward her.

I tried to speak, but when I opened my mouth no words came out. I swallowed, and finally I manage to stammer a reply, "It's okay. It's over now." In a blink of an eye, she disappeared.

"Evans, Evans," Alex was shaking my shoulders. "I'm getting you out of here."

I don't remember leaving the building. I remember Alex trying to speak to me while we were in the car. I didn't—or couldn't—hear him. I was stuck again in one of my moments where I just check out. When I finally came out of it, we were pulling up to the front entrance of our own building.

"Are you going to be all right?" He had a look of concern.

"Ye...yes," I said, and I got out of his car. I walked into the lobby and headed straight to the bathroom. I splashed water on my face, which helped me wake up. *It's not a big deal, Lyla. Stop overacting.* I sent Beck and David a text that I was coming over after work. I didn't want to be alone tonight.

When I walked out of the bathroom, I was surprised to see Alex. I hadn't anticipated that he would wait for me. He was leaning on the wall next to the bathroom door and he said, "Evans..."

I gasped. "Shit! Sorry, Ale...Mr. St. James, you startled me."

"Alex is fine. What did you see back there that got you so disturbed?"

"I...I...I've just never seen a dead body so close before." I took a breath and smiled. "You know, except at funerals." I'd been hiding my secret for so long that it was just natural for me to lie about it. The idea of saying, "I see dead people" aloud just seemed ridiculous to me. Not to mention my fear that whomever I said it to would look at me like I belong in an institution.

Alex looked me over. "I see. I'm sorry I brought you there. Can I take you home?"

"No, that's okay. I'll manage. Thank you." Without looking back, I walked to my car.

I drove straight to Beck and David's apartment. We ordered takeout and I played with my dinner. I stayed with them to watch TV until I couldn't keep my eyes open anymore. David drove me home. Without my having to ask, he offered to sleep on the couch. He could tell I was scared to be alone.

An hour into my sleep, I had a dream. I expected it. The feeling of dread was similar to sitting in a dentist's chair and knowing the dentist was about to start drilling.

"Lyla, Lyla, wake up. You're having a dream." When I finally woke up, I couldn't breathe. I was having a panic attack and I was trying hard to breathe.

"Try to take small breaths." David turned on the light next to my bed. It was a few minutes before I could breathe normally again.

"I'm okay. Why are you holding your face?"

"You smacked me," he said, still managing to give me a smile.

"What?"

"Hell of a dream you were having there. I'll get you some water and some ice for me."

"Don't leave me."

"I'll be back. I promise." David whistled as he walked away. It was his way of comforting me, letting me know that he wasn't leaving me alone.

When he came back, he handed me a glass of water. "Here, drink this." I did, and I placed the glass on my nightstand. David picked up the ice in my glass and pressed it on his face. "I don't think it was your usual 'Oh, shit, there's a blade sticking out of my stomach' dream. Did you have a different dream?"

"A nightmare, I think. I can't remember anything now."

"You'll remember when you want to." I looked at him, hoping he would see that I needed him close to me tonight. "I'll sleep on the floor. My back has been aching lately anyway. If anyone asks, I got this bruise from defending a girl at a bar, okay?"

"Thanks, David." I listened to David's breathing and eventually fell asleep. I heard my alarm go off and got out bed, following my morning routine like a zombie. I noticed that while I was taking a shower and making coffee, David moved to my bed. Before I left, I squeezed his hand and whispered, "Thank you."

chapter

SEVEN

Lyla

When I walked into the lobby, Simon greeted me. "Good morning, Lyla. They are waiting for you in the conference room." He led me to the elevators.

"Who's waiting for me, Simon?" He didn't answer but reached in and pressed the elevator button for me. "I'm here if you need me," he said as I stepped in the elevator.

I walked into the massive conference room just as someone said, "She has the gift." Riley and Lupe looked up and watched as I made my way to an empty seat, still unsure if I was supposed to be in here.

As I sat down, Riley resumed the conversation, "Of course she has the gift. Father has never been wrong about this. Some people have gaydar, Father has...well, he's just never been wrong."

"Who has the gift?" I asked confused.

"Well, you do, silly, and you've been keeping it a secret from us." I panicked. *How did they know my secret?*

"What do you mean I have the gift?" I asked.

"I knew she was one of us. I can smell them a mile away." Lupe slid her chair next to me and gave me a hug.

Alex walked in, still wearing the clothes he had on the day before. His hair was disheveled. Apparently he didn't always shower before leaving the house or maybe he never went home.

Riley got up and walked over to Alex. "The smell of human sweat and blond hair...let me guess, you paid a visit to your old girl-friend," Riley said quietly to Alex as he picked up a strand of blond hair from Alex's shirt. Alex swatted his hand away. "How is the old girl? Still a man eater?"

I don't know why I was starting to get a bit upset. I was get-ting irritated at myself for feeling wounded at what I heard. Who cared if he went to see his girlfriend? I certainly didn't...it was none of my business. *He's just my boss and nothing else.*

"I don't understand. What gift do you mean and how am I one of you?" I glanced over at Lupe.

"Hmm, either she still wants to keep secrets from us or she re-ally doesn't know," Riley responded.

"What are you trying to say?" I replied harshly. I was surprised at my reaction. I could feel myself getting defensive. Either my lack of sleep or the fact that this guy always annoyed me wasn't helping me to stay very patient.

"Calm down. I guess she really doesn't know anything." Riley sat down in the chair closest to mine and moved my chair to face him. "Let me explain; I think you might need some caffeine to keep up." He looked over to Lupe and nodded.

Lupe walked out of the conference room. I looked up at Alex, who was leaning by the window with his arms crossed over his chest. I tried to make eye contact, but he seemed more fascinated with his shoes. I felt silly; it was a desperate attempt to feel safe because I had a gut feeling my life was about to change drastically. I was scared, and I wanted someone to protect me. I suddenly missed my dad very much.

The blond receptionist walked in with four cups of coffee on a silver tray. She placed a cup in front of each of us. I think she actually flashed me a smile. She walked over to Alex, but he declined, "No thank you, Amanda."

Amanda…is that her name? It didn't escape my notice that Alex called her by her first name, something he never did with me. Just as quietly as she walked into the room, Amanda left.

As soon as the door closed, Riley spoke up, "Alex told us that you saw something unique at the crime scene."

I looked at Alex, but his expression never changed, so I turned to face Riley to try to explain. "I thought I saw something, someone that is, but it was just my imagination, that's all, really. I've never been at a crime scene before, and I guess my imagination went on overdrive. It's really nothing."

"Thou protest too much, I think." Riley caught on that I was bullshitting.

It was Lupe's turn to speak. "Listen, honey, no one is going to judge you. If you have a gift that can help solve these murders," she hesitated before she continued talking, "well, don't you think you should try to help? They're just innocent little girls, Lyla. They can't even defend themselves."

Just like that, her words hit me as if I was punched in the gut. "It's not that I don't want to help, but I don't even know what I saw. Maybe it was just my imagination."

Alex spoke for the first time. "Why don't you tell us what you think you imagined?"

"Fine." I took a deep breath and prepared to be called crazy. "I thought I saw a little girl. She was asking me for help."

"What did the little girl look like?" Riley asked.

I closed my eyes and tried to describe the little girl as best as I could. A wave of sadness replaced the guilt that had settled in my stomach. My mind was beginning to go blank.

Alex's voice brought me back. "Did she say anything else to you? Anything about the person who killed her?"

"No, it was very brief. My visions...or feelings...are usually very brief." I couldn't understand why I suddenly felt I had to defend myself. "Yesterday, was the first time that I actually communicated with...um...someone who wasn't alive anymore." I struggled for words.

"What do you mean?" Alex asked.

"Usually, I just have a feeling, just a feeling of a presence of someone who died in a place that I happen to be. I've never had anyone actually talk to me."

"So it is usually just a feeling?" Riley repeated my words slowly.

"And then," I paused and looked at my hands. "and then I have a dream of what happened to them, usually that same night or the next night."

"Did you have a dream last night?" Lupe asked, flashing me one of her warm smiles.

"Yes, but in the last few years it's changed. Lately I forget my dreams almost immediately. By the time I wake up, I don't remember the details, just that I had a dream."

Lupe's face looked disappointed as she confirmed that she heard me correctly: "Gone?"

"You don't remember anything about your dream last night?" Riley asked to clarify.

"No, I'm sorry. As I got older, I stopped remembering my dreams, except for this one particular dream that I keep having."

Riley pressed the intercom. "Bring Dr. Jenskee into the conference room right away."

An awkward silence was beginning to build up in the room as we waited for the doctor that Riley had summoned. It was Lupe who finally spoke up. "It might be silly to ask, but can you *try* to remember?"

I closed my eyes and opened them again. "Nothing. I'm so sorry. I do know that I woke up screaming, 'Stop! Stop!' to someone and I was fighting someone off."

Alex asked, "How do you know that?"

"David, I mean a friend of mine, told me that I was yelling 'stop' and that I accidentally hit him."

"Why Lyla, you didn't tell us that you were currently cohabitating," Riley raised his eyebrows.

"Cohabitating? What? No, and I don't think it's any of your business." I felt my cheeks burn.

"Actually, it is." Riley was interrupted mid-sentence by a knock. I was glad for the interruption. I didn't want to hear the rest of what Riley was going to say. An elderly man walked in. Riley looked at me before getting up. "But we'll discuss that at another time." He shook the man's hand and said, "Dr. Jenskee, thank you for joining us. This is Lyla Evans; she has a gift." Riley filled him in about my gift as well as my inability to remember my dreams.

"It is completely understandable. Forgetting the dreams is most likely Ms. Evans's way of coping with her abilities and still trying to maintain a normal human life," Dr. Jenskee explained.

Alex interjected, "So she forgets in order to pretend to be normal." I looked at him. His words really stung me. I felt like he was accusing me of being a coward and a fake.

The doctor left, and I felt like I had to defend myself again. "I *am* normal; it was just a dream or my mind overloaded. It must be all this research I've been doing. It must have just seeped into my subconscious." I gripped the arms of my chair to get up, but Riley put his hands over mine, causing me to sit down again. He passed me a file, and I opened it. Inside, there were photos of all the victims; I took my time, looking at each picture. All the girls looked like they were just sleeping. I closed my eyes and an image of a girl flashed vividly in my head. I knew instantly it was the same girl who was in my dream last night. *Weird, I finally started remembering my dreams again*. The girl in my dreams didn't match any of the pictures. I was relieved. It *was* just a dream, my imagination playing overtime.

Riley said what I was thinking. "The girl you described wasn't one of the victims." He paused for a second and then continued, "until this morning." He pulled out his cell phone, clicked a button, and slid it over to me. A picture of the girl I had seen in my dream was on his phone, except the girl on the phone was posed in the same way the other victims were.

I looked at Riley, not bothering to glance at Alex. Quietly, I said, "I don't understand."

"This photo was taken two hours ago. We just found the body."

"Two victims, one day apart...he's never done that before," I whispered to myself.

Alex, who had not moved from his spot by the window, asked, "How do you know the perpetrator is a male?"

"In my dream, I was fighting a male, early fifties maybe, with patches of gray hair. But he was strong." I gasped, realizing that I'd just remembered something else from my dream again. "The girl I described earlier was from my dream last night and not the same girl I saw at the crime scene. This is the girl who made her presence known to me yesterday." I pointed at one of the pictures on the table. Then I tapped the screen on Riley's phone, "This is the girl I saw in my dream last night. I must have gotten them confused. I really don't understand. I have only ever dreamed of people who passed away. Did I just dream about someone who wasn't dead yet?"

chapter

EIGHT

Alex

My brother took a breath and begin to explain. "Lyla, you're a Somnium: someone who sees visions during sleep; and in your case it sounds like when you are awake as well, which I've never heard of anyone being able to do. You can see things that happened as well as what *might* happen." Riley paused. He must have seen the blank stare on Lyla's face. "Let me start from the beginning. We are part of a small population of human beings who have been given a gift by God. When Lucifer fell, God saw that the balance was being tipped toward the side of Evil. To restore the balance, he gave a handful of humans special abilities to fight off Evil."

"Wait. You expect me to believe this?" Lyla asked in disbelief.

"Have unusual things been happening to you since you turned eighteen? You feel stronger, your reflexes are faster, and perhaps your dreams have been different." Lyla didn't respond.

"History is filled with people who have these special gifts: Joan of Arc, Harriet Tubman, and Mother Theresa, for example. History is also filled with people who have Pure Evil in them, like Genghis Khan, Adolf Hitler, and Charles Manson. Lyla, are you still with me?" Lyla's face was blank, unreadable.

"I think so, but why did you name only females on the 'good' side?"

"Of all the things I told you, you decided to question my list of examples." I didn't respond and just looked at him and shrugged my shoulders. "Well, actually, there are far more male heroes than female, but I didn't want to highlight that." Riley ended his sentence with a smile.

Lyla challenged him. "Name another, preferably male."

"To name just one would be impossible." Riley and Lupe looked at each other. "All right, Alexander the Great."

In a heartbeat, she responded, "He believed he was indestructible and often put his life at risk, as well as the lives of his soldiers."

"So he's not perfect. What about Napoleon Bonaparte?"

"He annulled his marriage with his first wife because she couldn't produce an heir, then he went on to marry the daughter of the Austrian Emperor. Not to mention the term, Napoleon Complex, was named after him."

"All right, he had self-esteem issues. Who doesn't? Che Guevara?"

"He ordered prisoners to be executed without a trial."

"But he helped so many lepers—don't forget that. So they weren't perfect, where are you going with this?"

"I'm just trying to understand what it means to have this gift that you claim God bestowed on us to fight Evil. What does that really mean? So I dream of dead people. *So what?* How can I fight Evil with that?"

I could tell from the look on Lyla's face that she was having a hard time believing who she really was. "There are many different types of gifts, Evans," I said quietly. I didn't move from my position by the window.

"Let just say mine is persuading people to do what I want them to do," Riley added with enthusiasm. I could sense that he was very excited that Lyla was one of us, almost glad that she, too, had a gift. "My father can make you see what he wants you to see. And you can see what people have done in the past or what they will do in the future. Don't you realize how big that is? You can help prevent people from getting hurt. Your gift allows you to save so many lives."

Lyla quickly turned to Lupe and asked, "What is your gift?"

"I can make anyone feel calm. Sort of like taking a Xanax."

"That can come in handy. Are you making me feel calm right now?"

"No, girl. It's kind of scary how calm you are right now."

Lyla looked up and faced me, "Do you have super strength as well?" Seeing her face caught me off guard. It was quick, but she showed me how scared she truly was.

"Yes, we are faster and stronger than the average human being." Riley put an emphasis on his words as he pointed to himself and to me.

"Michael Phelps, does he have a gift?" Lyla asked lightly and quickly, changing her facial expression.

"Good question, girl. I've wondered as well!" Lupe laughed.

"No, I think he's just a fast swimmer," Riley answered with very little interest in the subject.

"And you." She stared straight at me. "Let me guess: you read people's emotions?"

"Impressive." Riley responded. "Beauty and brains, but the ultimate question is, can she cook?" I remained silent, wondering if she already resented me for having the ability to invade her privacy.

"And this company, is it just a front?" Lyla continued to look at me, and I continued to study her facial expressions. They were all very brief, but at least they told me what she was feeling. Right now, she was beginning to feel betrayed for being lied to.

"Damn, you really are smart. Commercial real estate provides us with two things. One, it pays the bills, and two, once we acquire the building, we are free to investigate." Again, it was Riley who answered her questions, and I was glad for it. My mind began to wander to the fact that she wasn't alone last night.

"You think the psycho who has been killing all these little girls is, what, a..." Lyla struggled to find the proper term.

"We call them Pure Evil. Some say they are descendants of fallen angels that Satan dispatched on Earth and they literally have evil in their hearts. They have no remorse, and their only goal is to do harm. And yes, they too are stronger and faster than the average human. As far as we know, they do not have any other special gifts similar to ours. What we do know is that they are very driven to harm humans. They believe that it will please Lucifer and make them closer to him when they do go to hell, sort of like racking up points before they die." With a dramatic flair, Riley added the last sentence: "To hurt others is their main purpose during their life here on earth."

"Why does it have to be innocent little girls?"

"This particular Pure Evil likes little girls. It's the same as, say, you preferring chocolate."

"Why can't he prefer convicts, rapists, or other evil people in the world?"

"Some do. Why do you think there's such a high rate of men getting raped in jail?"

"Lyla prefers vanilla, and that's enough for today." I could tell by her facial expression that this conversation was getting too much for her to handle. I was starting to resent that I couldn't sense any of her feelings and I had to rely on her facial expressions. I grabbed her by the wrist and led her out of the room. She didn't say anything and just followed.

We were in my car before she finally spoke. "I'm glad to be out of that room. Thank you."

"Where do you want to go? I'll take you anywhere." I didn't need to sense her feelings to know that she felt completely lost. Her small voice conveyed that she suddenly felt very small against the world. I wanted so badly to hold her and tell her that she wasn't alone.

"Home. I just want to go home, please," she said. I nodded. In the end, all I could do was drive her home. I pulled up in front of her apartment building. I was about to get out of the car when she turned to say, "Thank you for taking me home. I don't think I could have driven myself. I appreciate it."

"I know it's a lot to take in, the feeling of being responsible for protecting the whole world. I know you must have a million questions," I paused to look at her face, "so feel free to call me, and I'll try my best to answer your questions." *Did I just say something as lame as feel free?*

She nodded and got out of the car. I watched her enter her building and drove straight to my father's house. When I pulled up the driveway that curved around the front of the house, I noticed his Rolls Royce waiting outside with the engine running. Phil, my father's chauffer, was waiting outside.

"Morning, Phil."

"Good morning, sir."

I quickened my pace up the grand stairs leading to the front door. My father's butler opened the door before I could pull the rope to ring the doorbell.

"Good morning, Tom."

"Good morning, Alex. It's good to see you."

"You as well. Is Father in his study?"

"Yes, he was just about to leave."

"Right." I glanced back at Phil and the car.

"Would you like me to have the chef fix you some breakfast, sir?"

"No, thank you. I just stopped by for a quick word with Father."

"Of course. I'll let him know." Tom began walking down the hall. His steps were slower than I remembered.

"That's okay, old man." I patted him on the shoulder as I moved past him. I found Father standing behind his desk. He was just about to close his attaché. He has been using the same one since I was a kid, and he saw me looking at it. "What can I say, I'm a sentimental man. Your mother gave this case to me as a present," he explained, tapping his finger on the handle of his attaché. "Alex, what a pleasure it is to see you. I'm pleasantly surprised, and I'm hardly ever surprised."

"I want to know more about the girl."

"Indeed, two mornings in a row inquiring about our dear Ms. Lyla Evans."

"Come on Father?" Riley gets his sense of humor from my father.

He motioned for me to sit down at one of the wingback chairs facing his desk. He placed the attaché down on the floor and sat down in his chair. He picked up the phone to tell Phil he would need a few more minutes. "Would you like something to drink, my dear boy?"

"I would like some answers."

"All right then. Let's get to it. I heard that Ms. Evans was debriefed about her unique qualities and that she took it rather calmly."

"Word travels fast."

"You should know that. I also heard that you visited a certain demon last night."

"I didn't think you entertained rumors, Father. You can't deny that she's the best resource we have to obtain information about our enemies."

"Let's not argue so early in the morning. Did you find out anything?"

"You first."

"Fair enough," Father responded. "I've known about Lyla for quite some time, and I suspected she had the gift, or rather, as it turned out, gifts."

"How, though? She didn't show up on our list."

"My dear boy, not everything can be Googled. It is our responsibility to keep track of certain bloodlines."

"I've never heard of or met someone with her abilities."

"She's very rare indeed, and she may come in very useful. Imagine the ability to prevent an atrocity before it happens." Father leaned in. "We can't lose her."

"There's just one problem; she has made herself forget about her dreams."

"Yet more often than not, one remembers a dream right after it occurs."

"What are you saying?"

"I'm saying that *your* gift is the perfect solution to the problem. You can read her feelings enough to know when she has a dream and she can tell you right away about her dreams."

"She lives on the other side of town. Have you forgotten that I need to be in the same room to read someone?"

"I'm told that you have a big house. Although I don't remember ever being invited, so I can't be sure."

"You want her to stay with me?" I purposely ignored his last sentence.

"Son, her life is in danger. If the enemy found out we have someone with her abilities, well, you can imagine that they would want to eliminate her right away."

"Why does she need to stay with me? We can assign a team to watch her."

"Yes, we could do that. But who else would know that she was having a dream?"

Her friend would, some guy named David would. Just thinking about his name made me agitated. "Don't," I warned my father.

"Don't what?" he asked innocently.

"You don't need to put a visual in my head of Lyla getting hurt. I get the point."

"You make me proud. You have mastered your gift far more than I expected. Do visit more often, Son. However, for today, I think we have let Phil wait for me long enough." I stood up and my father walked around his desk toward me. I was surprised when he hugged me and even more surprised when he whispered, "Do this old man a favor, and please take care of her."

My father must have seen the confusion on my face. I could count the number of times he has hugged me in my lifetime, let alone asked me for a favor that included the word *please.*

"I feel responsible for her. She thought she was signing up for research." He smiled and shrugged. I had a feeling there was a lot more that he wasn't telling me. He placed one hand on my back and led me out of his office.

Father has an uncanny way of explaining any situation in a believable way. I sometimes wonder if he has the power of persuasion just like Riley. Still, I couldn't deny the fact that father was right, my gift as an Empath was a perfect match for Lyla's abilities. I could sense when she had a vision because I could feel her emotions. But how was I going to explain to my father that I might not be the best person to watch over Lyla because my feelings had been compromised? *I am attracted to the woman I'm supposed to protect.*

chapter

NINE

Lyla

I never called him. I climbed into bed telling myself I would deal with it tomorrow. I watched every movie version of *Pride and Prejudice* until my eyes could no longer stay open.

I woke up the next day to the horrible noise of my alarm clock. I had the same feeling I did the morning after my first car accident when I was a teenager. I felt horrible, but slowly I allowed myself to accept that it had happened, except yesterday wasn't a fender bender. *What was yesterday?* I willed myself to get ready to go to work.

When I opened my door, I saw Alex standing outside, leaning on his car. He waved at me. I walked over and he placed a cup of warm coffee in my hands. "You didn't call," he said.

"I didn't have any questions yet," I replied.

He opened the car door, took my bag off my shoulder, and motioned for me to get in. "And today?" he asked as he started the ignition.

"I might have a question or two."

"Good," he replied. "I know the perfect spot for a Q & A." He drove to Old Town Pasadena. We got out of the car and walked along the streets. "I love it here in the mornings when the shops are still closed and there is hardly anyone around." I took a sip of my coffee.

We walked a few more blocks. At one point, he walked a little farther than me and sat on a bench. He patted the space next to him. I sat down. "So tell me, what are you most curious about?"

"Is it a burden to know what everyone feels?"

"What?" He chuckled. "That's what you're most curious about? *My* abilities?" He paused for a second. "I've learned to control it. I can turn it off and on."

I sensed that he wanted to say something else but was holding back. "What? What is it?"

"It's hard to read you." I gave him a blank look. I wasn't sure what he meant. "I can't read you, Evans. At first, I thought I was getting rusty then I realized that you are just able to control your feelings better than most."

I shrugged. "I scored very high on emotional intelligence. Self-regulation—it's an important quality in a leader." I gave him a fake grin.

He smiled back and leaned over closer to me so that our foreheads almost touched. "Evans, you have built walls so high that—"

"That what?" I interrupted him. "On second thought, don't bother answering. Do we have a name for ourselves? Avengers? Super Friends?" The blank look that he gave me told me that my joke was lost on him. *What a waste of a good line.*

"The only formal name we have been able to trace is linked to the Japanese Samurai warriors. Our research indicated that Japan was the first and only country to unite people like us with special gifts. So we have been identifying ourselves as Warriors."

"Is your mother a Warrior?"

"No, she wasn't. We don't know of any full-blooded Warrior who is still alive. My father is only half, his mother was a Warrior, and my brother and I are a quarter Warrior. As far as we can tell, our power doesn't diminish with less purity in the blood line. You just need to be a descendant of a Warrior. Although I think my grandmother has extraordinary powers—she always seems to know what Riley and I are up to. It certainly made it harder to sneak out of the house."

"Did you have a normal childhood?"

"As normal as can be given the fact that our father was running an organization devoted to hunting down Pure Evil. After school, most kids have soccer practice. We had training on how to control our abilities and stop and kill our enemies."

"What's going to happen to me now?"

"One day at a time, Evans. Today, you just focus on getting to know the real you." He held my hand and it felt nice. His hands were warm.

"A Somnium, or whatever it is you call me?" He nodded.

We were both quiet for a while. I watched a woman across the street walking her well-groomed Yorkie. "You must be really good in bed."

"What?" he asked choking on his coffee.

"If you can read or sense others' emotions and feelings, then you know exactly what your partner wants or needs."

Alex's cheeks turned a pale red. "I try not to abuse my powers." He looked away.

"Are you actually blushing? I'm sorry, that wasn't appropriate. I joke when I get nervous."

"You're a funny girl, Evans. Let's get some food in you. All I ever see you do is drink coffee."

That's weird. *How does he know I drink too much coffee*, I thought to myself. Alex let go of my hand and placed both his hands on my shoulders to turn me so that I was directly facing him. His facial expression turned grim, and in a stern voice, he told me, "Lyla, you need to wake up. Right now!"

"What?" My eyes flew open. I heard my heart racing. I was dreaming, but I realized that the sound of a window breaking wasn't part of my dream. Someone was in my apartment. Why did I turn down David's offer to stay over again? I reached for my cell phone. I got out bed slowly, trying not to make a noise. I placed my ear to the door. I could hear footsteps. *Oh God, there is someone in my apartment.* I checked my phone to see if any of the boys had sent a text or called to say they were coming over. No missed calls or texts. *Shit! Please, God, please help me!*

I was dialing 911 when the door swung open, hit me, and knocked me off my feet. In a matter of seconds, a man was on top of me and he pulled a knife from his back. Before my mind could register what had just occurred, I swung the hand that still held my cell phone as hard I could, across the man's face. I heard his nose break. He wasn't expecting my move, and he rolled to his side and held his face.

I pushed him off and got up as fast as I could, ready to run, but he recovered and held onto my legs, pulling me toward him. I hit the floor facedown, and for a moment I had the odd thought that this was the same fall I had taken the morning of my first day of work, which now seemed like centuries ago. I turned and kicked the man in the face. He fell on his back. I jumped on him, sat on his chest, and placed one of my knees on his neck. One of his hands tried to grab my neck, but I caught it in mid-air and slammed it hard on the floor. I heard the bones break, and relief almost washed over me. Except I was too late to see his other arm, which was still holding the knife, and I couldn't do anything except anticipate the knife plunging into me.

Suddenly, another pair of hands grabbed his wrist. My assailant dropped the knife, but whoever grabbed his wrist didn't let go and kept turning his arm all the way until it dangled out of the socket. My assailant screamed. I got off the man to get a better look at who had come to help me. I was baffled that I wasn't surprised to see Alex. In fact, I had to stop myself from asking what took him so long. I was expecting him…but why?

"Are you okay?"

I nodded.

"I don't think so Evans," Alex looked concerned. You have blood dripping down the side of your face." I reached for my face and my fingers encountered a warm liquid. I looked at my hand and blood was on my fingertips. I realized that blood was covering the right side of my face, including my eye. *Maybe that's why I didn't see the knife.*

"Oh, I'm bleeding." Then my room slowly turned dark.

chapter

TEN

Lyla

When I opened my eyes, I was in a hospital room or a luxurious hotel room with medical equipment. There was an IV hooked to my arm. I was still wearing my tank top and pajama pants. A man in a white coat had his back to me. He turned around and said, "Oh good, you're awake. What an eventful evening you've had." It was the same doctor who had come into the boardroom earlier today...or was it yesterday.

"Am I in the hospital?"

"Yes, in the company's private wing, to be precise. You have a mild concussion." I tried to sit up. "Take it easy and try not to get up too fast." He put his hand gently on my shoulder.

"How long have I been here?"

"Just a few hours. Alex is—" As soon as the doctor said Alex's name, he walked in the room. "Alex, I was just mentioning to

Ms. Evans that you were outside." Alex stood in the farthest corner of the room. *Did he think I had some kind of communicable disease?*

He stayed in the corner watching as the doctor checked my pulse and temperature. When the doctor announced that he was done, Alex finally spoke. "Is she well enough to leave? She isn't safe here."

"Why, Edward? Did you piss off another vampire?" I replied, trying to lighten the mood in the room. The doctor and Alex gave each other puzzled looks.

"Perhaps I should check her vitals again," the doctor offered.

"That might be best," Alex replied.

"I'm fine. I was just making a pop culture reference. Sorry." The doctor believed me. After I answered a series of questions about my name, birthday, and address and demonstrated that I was able to name the current president, the doctor finally removed my IV and released me.

I must have sat up and swung my legs over the bed too fast, because I felt a little dizzy. In two big steps, Alex was at my side holding me up. "Thanks; I guess I should've listened to the doctor when he said to take it slow." I looked around for my shoes.

"Sorry, I didn't think about grabbing you a pair of shoes. I was more concerned about stopping you from bleeding to death."

"That's okay. I wouldn't want bloodstains on my Manolos. Sorry, I tend to—"

"Joke when you get nervous." Alex finished my sentence.

"Exactly," I rationalized that the line was familiar enough for him to guess what I was going to say. There was a moment of silence between us that accelerated quickly to an awkward moment. I was glad when an orderly came in with a wheelchair.

"I guess my ride is here." I smiled at the orderly. The man was heading in the opposite direction from the arrows that pointed the way to the main lobby. I finally figured it out. "Seriously, we have our own lobby?" No one replied. When the door leading to the outside slid open, a cold wind blew, giving me the chills. Alex handed me the dark hoodie he was wearing. I wasn't sure what to say, so I just accepted the jacket and said, "Thank you." I guess my concussion was wearing off, because I was focused enough to make a mental note of what he was wearing. His black fitted V-neck t-shirt made him look like he just walked off a Hanes package.

We were both quiet in the car. I couldn't stand the awkwardness anymore, and I finally broke the silence. "Would you mind taking me to my friends' apartment?"

Alex kept his eyes on the road. "I can't."

"It's not too far from my own apartment. It's actually a lot closer." More silence. "My apartment is fine, then." Even more silence. "You just missed the turnoff to my apartment." Alex finally turned his head slightly in my direction.

"You want to go back to your apartment, where there is a dead body lying on your bedroom floor?"

"No, I want to go to my friends' apartment, which is just a few blocks from my—wait, did you just say *dead body*?" Alex looked at me out of the corner of his eyes. "Did you kill him, my...intruder?" I took a deep breath and willed myself not to overreact. *8, 16, 24 32, say it more slowly, 40.*

"Your intruder? He wasn't just an intruder crashing your dinner party." *48, why do I always forget what comes after 48?* "He was hired to kill you. He wasn't going to stop until he finished the job." *49, 50, 51, 52, 53, 54, 55, 56.*

"Do you do this often? Stop by people's houses and kill their assailants?"

"No, it's not how I would like to spend my nights nor is it a hobby for me to kill people."

"I'm running out of names to properly identify that guy who broke into my apartment."

"Assassin. He was an assassin."

48, 56, 64. "Where are we going?"

"My house."

"Why your house?"

"Because you'll be safe there."

"To stay with a man who just killed a man and yet has made no indication that he needs to explain it to the police."

"To stay with someone who would protect you and prevent others from taking your life." *48, 56, 64, 72, and 80.* I took another deep breath.

"Won't the police want to know why there's a dead body in my apartment?"

"We took care of the body."

"So then there's no dead body in my apartment." He didn't reply, and we sat in silence for a while. "Why?"

"Why, what?"

"Why are you protecting me?"

"I was assigned to."

"I mean, why do I need protection? Why do people want to kill me?"

"Most likely because of your gifts."

"My gifts that I just found out about and that only you, your brother, and the people at the company I work for know about. What if it's *your* people who want me dead? I'm supposed to just go along with you and stay at your house? And wait, you said *gifts,* so I have more than one?"

"Do you analyze everything? We're not trying to kill you, Evans, but someone is. The same Pure Evil who hired the guy to attack you tonight will likely find another scum to hire and finish the job. If I wanted to kill you, I wouldn't have *saved* you, and I wouldn't take you to my house." Alex's voice was trailing off. I couldn't hear him anymore.

8, 16, 20...why can't I think anymore? I began to feel tired and could only manage a whisper when I asked Alex, "Why were you at my apartment?" My eyelids felt so heavy. I decided to close them for a second.

The last thing I heard was Alex calling my name, "Evans. Evans. Are you sleeping?" I couldn't answer him. "Finally, the meds kicked in." He sighed deeply.

chapter

ELEVEN

Alex

Lyla looked so small and fragile lying on the bed in the guest room. Light from the outside was beginning to filter into the room. It sickened me to think that she could have been seriously hurt—or worse—if it had taken me one more second to get to her. When I saw her assassin about to plunge the knife into her throat, I wanted to bash the guy's head in. Seeing her faint almost made my heart stopped.

I hoped she wouldn't see how ashamed I was that I almost failed to protect her. Kneeling next to the bed and holding her hand, I vowed never to fail her again. I closed my eyes realizing how emotional I had become. *Who was this girl to me anyway?* Still, it was my duty to protect her, and I couldn't shake the feeling that I was always supposed to protect her.

My only saving grace was that the night before I had listened to my gut feeling that something didn't feel right. I spent the evening driving around her neighborhood. I was just about to go home when I saw a shadow of a man enter her apartment building. I parked and jumped out of the car. There were broken pieces of glass by her patio door. I quickened my pace, knowing the man was already inside her apartment. Lyla must have tried to fight him off, but she didn't see the knife until it was too late.

I wasn't sure how long I had been staring at her face trying to memorize every feature, line and curve. She had the cutest nose I had ever seen and her lips were so full, I found myself wanting to feel them. At the very thought of this desire, I snapped to attention. *What the hell am I doing? This is ridiculous.* I ran my fingers through my hair chastising myself for allowing my thoughts to go in that direction. My second vow that night was to not let my emotions interfere with protecting Lyla.

My cell phone beeped, and I was glad for the interruption. It was a text from Lupe letting me know that the team I had assembled was five minutes away. I quickly changed and walked out my door just as an unmarked, small black Hummer pulled into the driveway. I pressed the button to open the garage door and motioned for the driver to pull in. I didn't want to take the chance that someone might notice the Hummer in the driveway, put two and two together, and figure out where Lyla was staying. She was right about one thing; only the people from the company knew about her gifts.

The sun had risen by the time Lupe, Simon, the security guard that Lyla had befriended, and two other men I had asked to be put on security detail jumped out of the vehicle. "Thanks for getting here so quickly," I said. I led them inside the house and motioned for everyone to sit at the dining table. It was time to discuss strategy. "What's the status on Lyla's apartment?"

"The body has been taken care of. The coroner is examining him right now. He'll call you as soon as his report is ready. The apartment has been put back together. We replaced the broken window. The tech department put all her contacts on her new phone as well as a tracking device like you asked." Lupe pulled out a cell phone and slid it over to me. "And here's the charger too."

A beeping sound came from the box on the wall in the kitchen. Simon and the other two men quickly jumped out of their seats to investigate. "It's okay; it's probably just Flora." I got up to check the screen. It was Flora. I pressed the button that automatically opened the front doors to let her in, meeting her at the door to debrief her about Lyla and the security team. Flora has been taking care of the St. James family since she moved here from the Czech Republic. She was used to the activities my family was constantly engaged in.

When I left home, Flora told my father that she would come to my house a few times a week to clean and to make sure I was eating properly. I told her that she didn't have to, but she insisted, stating firmly that she had promised my father she would always look after his children. She was repaying my father for saving her and her family from a Pure Evil who had a passion for DNA research and experimenting on live human beings.

Flora acknowledged the team with a slight nod. "I will make coffee and check on Ms. Evans." She went straight to the kitchen.

I returned to the table. Lupe got up from her seat and said, "I'm going to put her bags in her room."

I nodded and continued speaking with the rest of the team about where I wanted a pair of eyes at all times. I wasn't going to take chances with Lyla's safety again.

◖◗

Lyla slept most of the day. Flora agreed to stay and watch over her in case she woke up before I returned. Simon and his team were also watching Lyla and the house. At dusk, I decided to head to the LA River to meet Jane. If an assassin had been hired, she would know about it. Most likely, she got a cut for helping the deal along. I needed to know who wanted Lyla dead.

I entered one of the tunnels near the river, a place that usually went unseen by the public unless you knew what you were looking for. I hated this place, but it was a good start to find answers. A homeless man was lying just inside the mouth of the tunnel. I kept my eye on the man until I was past his reach. I knew better than to let my guard down until I was miles away from here.

I was near the chamber where I always met Jane, a dark and dank opening that led to several tunnels. A deep purple velvet chaise occupied the middle of the open space. Two men stepped out of the shadows. "What do you want, Warrior? Come to pay my mistress another visit?" The man opened his jacket and tapped on the butt of his gun.

"Care to let her know that she has a visitor?"

I heard a hissing sound from the side. "Now, now, boys, it's a little early for all this testosterone." Jane stepped out of the shadows. As usual, she was wearing something white. Today, it was a white jumpsuit and silver stilettos. She was almost my height. She walked over, lay down on her chaise, and flipped her blond hair back. She dismissed the two men with a wave of her hand. "Didn't you just pay me a visit not too long ago? Yet here you are again." Her lips slowly curled into a sardonic smile. "What a nice surprise, but clearly you haven't been gone long enough for me to really miss you." She curled her finger to motion me to come closer.

I walked over and stood over the chaise. I was getting impatient and went straight to the point. "An assassin was hired not too long ago to kill a young woman. Do you know anything about it?" She motioned for me to sit down. Reluctantly, I did and she crossed her legs and placed them on my lap.

"No flowers or chocolates, just a demand for what I know about a silly little girl." She leaned toward me, caressing my face with her fingers. Most men were attracted to Jane, with her long blond hair that went perfectly with her Barbie figure. However, most men didn't know what I knew, which was that Jane liked to play with and eat men's hearts, literally.

I didn't respond. I stood there watching her every move. My gut feeling told me something was different with Jane today.

"If I answer your question, what will I get in return?" Jane narrowed her eyes at me.

"Your menu." We studied each other intently. Jane and I had a long-standing deal. She would supply me with information and I would supply her with a list of names that we had identified as Pure Evil. It was a win-win. The men, evil or not, always fell for Jane.

Jane traced her finger along the side of my neck and down the base of my throat. "I bet you're tasty."

I shoved her legs off my lap. "Who hired the assassin?"

"I never met the person. I received a text of the girl's name and address and a nice little bonus for helping him or her find a man to do the job." She pulled out her cell phone, pushed a few buttons, and passed it to me. Lyla's picture was on the screen along with her address.

I handed the phone back to her. "Next time someone even mentions this girl's name, via text or otherwise, you let me know right away or our little deal is off and I'll cut your heart out and feed it to the rats in this hell hole." I got up to leave.

She grabbed my jacket, pulling me toward her until our faces were only inches apart. She was stronger than I had anticipated. "Hmm...interesting. I do believe that this girl has managed to worm her way into your heart." She moved my jacket aside and tapped her finger on my shirt, right over my heart. Smiling, she whispered, "Better be careful, Alex, you finally have a weakness." She moved her finger from my chest to her lips, my blood running down her index finger, and licked her finger. "Shh, don't let anyone know." I walked away, angry that I had let her get so close to me. The little cut she gave me over my heart felt like an annoying paper cut and I could hear her laughing and calling out to me, "I knew you would be tasty!"

chapter

TWELVE

Lyla

I woke up from a very deep, dreamless sleep. I was grateful for the restful night. When I opened my eyes, rays of orange light filtered through a room I didn't recognize. *Shit, why can't I remember anything?* I realized my memory was blank. I was starting to panic when I heard a tap on the door and a woman came in. It was Flora, the woman I had met at Alex's house.

"Oh, good, you're finally awake. You must be hungry." She carried a tray of food and placed it on the nightstand. "I've seen that look before; you don't know where you are." I shook my head. "Ms. Evans, you are at Mr. Alex St. James's house. He said you have concussion from your run-in with a man who was trying to harm you."

Flashes of fighting with the stranger quickly filled my head, as well as my brief stay in the hospital and the ride home to Alex's house. I took a deep sigh and winced as a wave of pain rolled from the back of my neck to the top of my head. "If you need anything, please let me know. The doctor has already visited while you were still asleep. He left some medication for your pain, but he said you must eat first before taking them. I made some chicken soup for you." My stomach rumbled at the sound and smell of the soup. She picked up the bowl of soup and handed it to me.

"May I have a drink of water first, please?"

"Of course, so polite. Someone raised you right."

"My father and a grumpy old Japanese man."

I felt a wave of embarrassment remembering how I had stormed into Alex's house the last time we'd met. "I apologize for the way I barged in last time." She laughed softly.

"I was glad to be able to witness it. It has been a long time since I have seen Alex react like a normal person." She laughed again. "Now eat, child."

I inhaled the soup, trying to slow down when Flora warned me about getting a stomachache from eating too fast. I ran my fingers through my hair; it was greasy. "How long have I been here?" I asked.

"Early this morning, and you have been asleep this whole time." She handed me my glass of water and two large pills.

"May I take a shower?"

"I'll draw you a warm bath. It will help you feel better," she said, examining my face. You will find everything you need in the bathroom. Your clothes have been put away."

She stood up and walked to the door that I assumed led to the bathroom. I got out of the bed. My legs felt like jelly, and I had to place my hand on the bed to steady myself. When I felt that my legs could hold me up, I walked around. The bedroom was big, bigger than a hotel room. There was a lovely wingback armchair and a footstool in the corner of the room by the bay window, and a dark mahogany desk and a chair on the opposite side. I walked over to the bay window. It was already dark outside, but I could hear waves. I wondered if there was a view of the ocean. I found the walk-in closet with my clothes organized the same way they'd been at my apartment. *Huh, that's convenient.* I walked over to the bathroom. "Most of my clothes are here, Flora. How long am I supposed to stay here?"

Flora looked up from her bent position next to the bathtub. "I do not know, Ms. Evans." With a smile, she said, "It is nice to have a guest in this house." She dipped her fingers in the water. "I put some Epsom salt in the bath for you." She dried her hands on a towel. "It will make you feel better. Do you need help getting in?"

"No, that's okay. I'll manage. Thank you, and please call me Lyla."

Flora gave me a small nod and left. I looked around the bathroom; it was two times bigger than my bathroom, maybe even three. The bathtub could easily fit two people. *I could get used to this.*

After my bath, I looked at my reflection in the mirror and realized what Flora had meant. There was a large bruise on my cheek. I flinched at my own touch. I must have gotten it when the door smacked my face, or maybe it was from landing facedown on the floor. I sighed and realized I was getting sleepy again.

Unfortunately, it was not a dreamless night. I kept reliving being attacked, but in my dreams, Alex wasn't there to stop the knife. I could hear a familiar voice whispering my name, telling me everything was okay and I was just dreaming. I also felt someone's warm hands holding mine and gently stroking my forehead. Feeling safe, I let my dreams unfold. It ended with my usual dream of a thin, long blade stabbing me in the stomach.

I woke up alone with no warm hands holding mine. Streams of light entered the room. I stretched my back. I was sore from lying down for so long. I took a shower and dressed in jeans, a cotton V-neck shirt, and my sweater that the boys have dubbed the "grandpa" sweater. I slowly made my way down the clear stairs, carefully placing my feet on the steps, still feeling unsafe without at least a railing to hold onto.

I was surprised to see Simon standing at the foot of the stairs. He was dressed in a black suit instead of his security uniform. We exchanged smiles. "Good morning, Ms. Evans. I'll be taking you to the office today. Breakfast is waiting for you in the kitchen." When I got closer to him, he tilted my chin and examined my face carefully. I thought I heard him mumble the word *bastard*.

"Good morning, Simon," I said dropping my face down. He let go of my chin and I followed him to the kitchen. There was a spread of various breakfast items on the large marble-topped island. "Wow, this is a lot of food."

"We weren't sure what you usually liked to eat for breakfast."

"Just coffee." I saw a frown on his face. "This smells so good, though. I think I'll have some of the omelet. Will you join me?"

He pointed to the food, saying, "But this is for you."

"Please, I hate eating alone."

"Well, okay. The bacon smells really good."

We cleared some space on the counter and ate together. I asked about Alex. Simon said that he had left an hour ago, instructing him to take me to the office when I was ready. He asked me about what had happened the other night. I recounted as much as I remembered. I asked him how long he'd been working for the company. He explained that his dad was head of security and retired not too long ago. As a young boy, he had always wanted to follow in his father's footsteps. Grinning, he explained that being assigned to my security team was his first field assignment. He was glad to get rid of the security uniform. With our glasses of orange juice, we toasted to his promotion. *Why do I have a security team?*

I washed our dishes and hurried up the stairs as fast as I could, grabbing my cell phone and purse. Simon led me to Alex's garage, where a small black Hummer was waiting. "Wow, who owns this many cars?" I said.

Simon smiled. "Mr. Alex St. James." We both laughed. I noticed that Simon was preoccupied while driving. His eyes were always looking around and checking the rearview mirror. I stayed quiet, figuring it was best not to distract him with questions. Instead of using the parking lot in the front, he drove around to the back of the building. A large metal gate rolled up as we pulled up. I noticed several cameras along the ceiling of the garage. As soon as we stopped, two men dressed in black suits that were similar to Simon's clothes walked up to our vehicle. One of the men opened my door, saying, "Good morning, Ms. Evans."

"Good morning."

"Follow me, please."

We walked along a series of hallways with cameras on the ceiling installed every few feet. There was an elevator at the end of the hallway. There were no panels or buttons inside. Once inside, I was surprised that we went down instead of up.

When the elevator doors finally opened, Lupe was waiting outside. Lupe gave me a hug and said, "I'm so glad you're okay."

"I'm fine. Where am I?"

"In the office." She winked. "Come on, they are waiting for you." I noticed she didn't give me one of her warm smiles.

"Who?" I asked.

"We call them the Scientists. Don't worry, it won't be too painful." Her face almost looked apologetic.

chapter

THIRTEEN

Lyla

I was ushered into a white and sterile room with medical equipment laid out. An elderly man in a white coat introduced himself to me. He had a deep accent, maybe English. "Hello, Ms. Evans. My name is Doctor Liam Rogets." I shook his hand, which was cold. "I'll be proctoring various exams today, all procedural of course."

He handed me a gown. I was glad it was cotton and not the paper towel that I usually get at my OB's office. "Lupe will stay with you throughout the exams."

"To make sure I stay calm?" I looked over to Lupe, who was sitting in the corner of the room. She wouldn't make eye contact with me.

"I heard you were a clever young lady." He patted my hand. I noted his heavy hands. "We will not do anything you do not want to do. I promise. Now let's get started. You can change over there." He pointed to a corner of the room with a modesty panel. I will step out and come back when you are ready." He pushed his eyeglasses up the bridge of his nose.

My gut screamed for me to bolt. I was surprised that my body stayed calm and followed all the directions the Scientist asked me to do. I tried to reason with myself that I shouldn't feel this calm, but Lupe's ability came in handy and I felt like I had taken a valium.

A mousy female assistant who was also wearing a lab coat took my vitals and a vial of my blood. Dr. Rogets placed ECG leads all over my body. I wasn't sure what he was measuring, but he stood by a machine and mumbled the word *interesting* every so often.

Two hours later, I was done. The assistant told me I could get dressed. Lupe was sweating; she looked worn-out. She quickly excused herself from the room. I hastily got dressed and stepped out from behind the modesty panel. Riley entered the room, picking up one of the metal instruments lying on the tray. "Are they done probing and prodding you?"

"I guess so," I said, putting my sweater back on.

"You must have fought hard. Lupe looks like she just ran a marathon." He flinched when he saw the bruise on my face.

"I don't know what you mean. I followed all their instructions."

"Hmm, come on. Let's get out of here. This room gives me the creeps."

I followed him out of the room and into another room that looked like the VIP waiting room at the airport. He handed me a glass bottle of water. I sat down on one of the couches, and Riley sat down next to me.

On the coffee table in front of us was a tray that held two carafes with beautifully etched labels noting that one was coffee and the other was tea. There were also elegant-looking cookies and white mugs and saucers. Steam was coming out of both carafes. Riley poured himself a cup of tea.

"How does it work, your abilities?" I asked him.

"I simply make suggestions." He took a sip of his tea.

"Okay, I'll give you three chances to get me to do something. Oh, I'm sorry, to *suggest* I do something."

"All right, but you have to promise to say out loud exactly what you are thinking and feeling."

"So you can try to figure out how my brain works."

"Exactly." He tried to hide a naughty smile.

"Game on, Riley." I smiled back.

"Lyla, you look a little bit tired."

I immediately wanted to yawn, but I stopped myself. "No, even with the bad dreams, I had way over eight hours of sleep last night, and eight hours is the recommended number of hours for your body to get enough rest and get reenergize." I emphasized the last word.

"Hmm, she's logical. I figured as much. Lyla, can I get you a cup of coffee?" In my head, I heard a voice telling me that I wanted a cup of coffee. *"It will help you stay focused and more alert."*

"No, thank you," I replied even though I really wanted one.

"I absolutely adore a girl who has so much control over her desires."

As Riley was talking, in my mind, I heard the same voice telling me to lean closer to him. It was tempting, like I just saw something in a store window that interested me, and without thinking I leaned closer to Riley.

"Lyla, you are attracted to me?" I wasn't sure if he was asking me or making a statement. I looked up at his face, such a handsome face with bright green eyes that I could stare at all day. "Yes."

He smiled.

"Wait, I mean *no*." I pulled back. "Well, of course I'm attracted to you, and you know that you're very handsome and attractive. So, yes, just by your physical attributes, anyone would be attracted to you." Pausing, I added, "But I chose not to be because—" Then that dreamy and alluring voice came into my head again, *"Kiss me."*

I stopped talking, tilted my head up, and felt his warm lips. I closed my eyes and asked myself, *What are you doing?* His lips felt soft and warm, and I could feel his arms around my waist and his hands on the small of my back. I answered by cradling his bottom lip deeper between mine.

Then came one word in my head, and I wasn't sure if Riley planted it in there or if I let myself think it: *Alex.*

I broke our kiss and put the palms of my hands on his chest. I tried really hard not to overreact that he had just stolen a kiss from me. To him, it was probably just a game. I smiled and said, "Okay, you got me." I glared at him, but he just smiled back.

I heard someone clear his throat. I quickly looked over in the direction the noise had come from. It was Alex, leaning on the doorway with his hands crossed in front of his chest. "Are you done, brother?"

Without looking up, Riley answered, "Baby brother, it's so nice of you to join us." I was just showing Ms. Evans my abilities."

"Come on, Evans, Father wants to meet you."

I stood up and followed Alex out of the room. I stopped when I reached the doorway and turned back to look at Riley. He was still watching me. In my mind, I said, "That was pretty low. We agreed that you would only try to make me do three things." I knew he wouldn't hear me, but it made me feel better to least say it in my mind. The shock on his face made me wonder if he did hear me after all.

chapter

FOURTEEN

Lyla

Alex didn't speak to me. I stared at his broad shoulders as I followed him. I told myself sternly that it would be inappropriate for me to look down any farther. I finally broke the silence when I lost my internal battle and found myself staring at Alex's firm butt. "Why does your father want to see me?"

"I'm not sure; probably to ask you about your research."

"Should I get my reports?"

"Fine," he sounded annoyed.

I was glad to see the hallway leading to my office. I felt like I had entered some twisted version of the Twilight Zone since Simon and I had entered at the back of the building and nothing had looked familiar. I walked into my office and immediately knew that someone had been in there. "I guess someone was here," I said, turning on my computer and punching in my password.

"What do you mean?" Alex asked stopping at the doorway.

I lifted a blue plastic Bic pen. "I don't use blue pens." Alex was fast; I barely noticed that he had entered my office when I found myself standing behind him. He looked around and checked under my desk.

"Anything else seem off to you?"

"No."

"You touched the keyboard already?"

"Yeah, I did, sorry."

"Check to see if any of your files are missing."

I walked back to my desk and clicked my mouse around to open my files. I looked up from the screen. "All my files are missing."

Alex bent to look at the screen. I clicked a few files to open to show him that they were all empty. He picked up the phone and barked, "Send Harris from the IT department." He looked at me and added, "Thank you," before placing the phone back on the cradle.

"That's a first," Alex told me.

"What?"

"That was the first time you've ever let me feel anything from you, and it was a mixture of annoyance and disappointment."

"Huh."

"So what are you annoyed and disappointed about?"

I kept my head down as I looked through my drawers to see if anything was missing and answered his question. "Since you're asking, you guys never say please or thank you. You go around ordering people to do things."

"You guys, meaning my brother and me?"

"It doesn't hurt to be polite."

"What do you really want to say?"

I was grateful to hear a knock on my doorframe. "Mr. St. James, you asked for me?"

"Yes—thank you for coming so quickly. All the files are missing from this computer. I want to know who did this and how someone was able to break through our firewall."

"Hi, Harris." I got up from my chair to get out of his way. Harris had helped me set up my username and password on my first day.

"Hey, Lyla. How's it going?" He sat in my chair and plugged his laptop into my hard drive.

"Did your wife have the baby yet?" I took a seat on the other side of my desk.

"Any day now," Harris replied, tapping the cell phone strapped to his belt.

Alex cleared this throat. "Did you find anything?"

"All the firewalls are still up. I don't see any virus. No failed log-in attempts." Harris looked up to face me, "Anything weird happen the last time you logged in or saved?"

"None that I can think of."

"I'll check the trash can." Harris hit a few more strokes on his keyboard and moved the mouse around.

"I'm sorry Mr. St. James. I'm not sure what happened here. But our firewalls, as you know, are impenetrable."

"Thank you, Harris." Harris unplugged his laptop and left.

I pulled out my cell phone. I had not checked it since that night in my apartment. I had thirty-three missed calls. I cringed at the thought of making David, Beck, and Lance worry unnecessarily about me. I quickly sent a group text to tell them I was okay, then I called Beck.

"Hi, Beck," I greeted him with a contrite voice.

"Are you okay?" I could hear panic in his voice.

"Yes."

"Are you sure?"

"I swear on your collection of Transformer Action Figures that I am."

"Okay, hold on. Let me pull the APB that I put out on you.

"What?"

"I was worried, okay. It's not like you to go MIA and not answer our calls or texts."

"Take if off before I get pulled over."

A few seconds later, he replied, "Done…so why did you go off the grid?" Beck finally relaxed.

"I'm sorry. It's a long story but I'm really okay. I need a favor."

"Shoot."

"Is there any way you can check to see if someone hacked into my computer at work?"

"Besides me?"

"You hacked into my computer?" Alex pulled the phone out of my hands and pressed the button for the speakerphone.

"Of course. I gotta tell you that your firewalls are off the charts. Props to your IT department. It's been one of my hardest ones to break into, but I did it." Beck did his evil laugh. "No one can stop the Beckster. Hey, am I on speakerphone?"

"Yes," I replied quickly.

"Oh," Beck replied in a small voice.

"What did you find?" Alex asked in a firm voice.

"Lyla, is that your boss?"

"Uh, yeah?"

"Well, uh, I don't usually make a habit of hacking into private systems, but my friends and I were worried about Lyla and I just wanted to check if she went to work yesterday. You know what I mean?"

"You could have just called the office and asked if she was at work," Alex replied.

"That's definitely one way." Beck was quiet for a second. "Am I going to get in trouble for this?"

"Not if you tell me what else you found."

"Oh, why didn't you just say so? Someone logged in and tried to copy all of Lyla's files last night at exactly 11:48 p.m. I figured that wasn't you, Lyla, so I stopped him—or her, I'm not gender biased—and placed your files somewhere else for safe keeping."

"You breached our firewalls?"

"I know right? Practically the best I've seen. At first I thought, wow, I finally met my match, but then I realized I couldn't break in from the outside, but what if I was already inside? I mean, I had to go 'old school' to tap in."

"What are you talking about, Beck?" I asked.

"Yesterday afternoon, I went to your building, pretended I was the cable guy, and plugged in, then the walls came magically down. I've been monitoring it ever since."

"Are you saying the person who hacked into Lyla's computer did it from inside our building?"

"Yup. Hey, Lyla, do you want your files back? I'll save them on a flash drive."

"Um, sure."

Alex was on his cell phone before I could say goodbye to Beck. I assured Beck that I was fine and safe. I also promised that I would contact David and Lance to let them know what had happened. When I looked up, Simon was at my doorway.

"Please take her home, Simon." Without saying anything to me, he left the room.

chapter

FIFTEEN

Alex

After speaking with Father and Riley about the possible security breach in our company, I spent the rest of the day and most of the evening sifting through the surveillance video. Like me, my father and Riley refused to believe that anyone would betray the company. But eventually we accepted the possibility that the attack on Lyla and the inside job of hacking into her computer all led to someone who was one of us. My father felt betrayed and didn't even try to hide his feelings from me.

After midnight, I gave up searching through personnel files for anything out of the ordinary. Anyone could have done it, but the question was why? *Besides a Pure Evil, who sees Lyla as a threat?*

I stopped by Lyla's room before heading into mine. She was asleep. Her laptop was still playing a video. It was Lyla as a little girl on a swing being pushed by her father. "Higher, push me higher!"

Lyla giggled. Lyla's face was angelic even as a little girl. I turned off the video and closed her laptop. Lyla stirred. I could feel a sense of panic. She was dreaming again.

"Lyla, it's okay. You're just dreaming." I held her hand. "You're safe. I promise."

I could hear Lyla's heart beating faster. Whatever was happening in her dreams, Lyla was scared. I continued to hold her hand and whispered that she was safe. When her dreams ended, Lyla's eyes flew open and she jumped into my arms. I didn't want to let her go. I could feel her chest rising quickly up and down, "Breathe, Lyla. You need to breathe, slowly." A few moments later, she dropped her arms and pulled back. I felt a wave of embarrassment.

"Sorry, I thought you—" She tried to speak, but she was still trying to get her breathing back to normal.

I interrupted her. I didn't want to know who she mistook me for. "I'll get you some water." I poured her a glass of water from a pitcher that Flora had left in her room. "Here," I offered her the glass. "Did you have a dream?"

"Yes."

"Can you tell me what it was about?" She didn't respond. "I'll tell you what I know. Whatever your dream was about, you were scared, and you were running." This prompted her to speak.

"I was in a large warehouse. Someone—no, more than one, maybe two men or even three, I can't remember. But we were being chased or led."

"We?" I asked, and Lyla closed her eyes.

"I don't remember." She opened her eyes again. "It was hot and very sunny. Open space...I wasn't in the city."

"Maybe the desert?" I asked.

"Yes, the desert, definitely."

"Anything else?"

"Motorcycles, I could hear a lot of motorcycles." She paused and looked up at me, "That's it; that's all I can remember."

"Have you had this dream before?"

"No, I've never had this dream, never."

"Try to go back to sleep, Evans." I took the glass of water from her hands, placed it on the nightstand next to her bed, and walked out of her room feeling helpless.

chapter

SIXTEEN

Lyla

I woke up the next morning feeling embarrassed. The first thought that came into my head was hugging Alex last night. I groaned and thrashed my legs and arms on the bed. *Why, why, why did I hug him? Why did I hug my boss? What's wrong with me? Wait, did he call me by my first name?*

There was a knock on my door. Flora walked in. "Good morning, Lyla. You look better. You can hardly see the bruise." She walked over to the bay window and pulled the curtains to the side. "I have breakfast ready for you downstairs."

"Is Alex awake yet?"

"He already left." Flora must have seen a puzzled look on my face. "He told me to let you sleep in."

"Am I going into the office today?"

"No, he said you need to stay home." Flora gave me a stern look.

"I can't leave the house?"

"It is for your own safety." Flora gave me a smile and left the room.

I showered, dressed, and went downstairs. I was proud of myself for going a bit more quickly down the clear steps. My fear was easing back a little. I didn't see Simon anywhere. I could smell food in the kitchen. I was glad to see that the spread wasn't as elaborate as yesterday's. I made myself a plate and stared at the door. I wondered what would happen if I just walked out. *I'm not a prisoner being held here against my will...or am I?*

Between bites of my egg white with spinach, I walked over to the door and found it locked, except that there were no visible locks, just a door handle. "Did you need something, Ms. Evans?" The voice startled me. I gave a small scream. A man in a dark suit, similar to the one Simon wore, was standing behind me.

"You scared me. Where did you come from?"

"From that room, he pointed to a door off to the side. My apologies for startling you, Ms. Evans."

"I wanted to see if there was a newspaper outside. Can you open the door so I can check?"

"No, I can't do that. Will the *LA Times* be sufficient?" I nodded. He started to talk into a gadget strapped on his wrist.

Feeling guilty about my lie, I stopped him. "That's okay; I'll just catch the news on TV." He turned to head back to the room he had come out of. I stopped him and asked, "Am I not allowed to leave?"

"It's for your own safety." He went around me and stood in front of the door.

"I heard that before." I walked back to the kitchen to finish my breakfast that I no longer had an appetite for. Maybe I shouldn't have told the boys that I was safe. I was trying to sort out my thoughts with the realization that I had no free will to walk out of this house.

I sat on the couch and played around with the remote control, not really paying attention to the screen. I heard Riley's voice by the door. He was speaking to the man who stood between the outside world and me.

"Morning, sunshine," Riley said as he walked over and sat down on the couch next to me. "Are they treating you all right here at Casa del Alex?"

"Why can't I leave?"

"What do you mean?" I tilted my head toward the man standing at the door.

"Ah, Alex does tend to go overboard. He likes to keep his precious possessions safe."

"Possessions." As much as I was glad to see a familiar face, Riley just bugged me. My gut twisted remembering our kiss.

"You want out, let's go. We'll go for a drive." He winked.

"Okay, but stop winking at me." I agreed to leave with Riley, hoping that on the way back I could persuade him to drop me off at Beck and David's apartment. "Let me grab my purse."

On our way out, the man stepped in front of Riley. "Sorry, sir, but my direction is not to let Ms. Evans out of the house."

"Out of the house alone, sure. But she's with me, so it's fine." The man walked over toward a panel on the wall that slid up with a wave of his hand. There was small black box with a key pad, and he punched in the code and opened the door for us. So that's how you open the door. Right, because a simple lock on the door would be too complicated.

"Have a great day, Mr. St. James, Ms. Evans," The man nodded slightly at each of us.

"Did you use your Jedi mind trick?" I asked Riley. I felt bad for the guy. He would have to explain to Alex why he let me leave the house.

"A *Star Wars* reference, I like it."

"How come you get my pop culture references, but your brother never does?"

"Alex? He's just boring. Growing up, all he did was train, train, train. I think he was fixated on avenging my mother's death." I didn't reply. I wasn't sure what to say to that. Riley led me to his black Audi. He opened the passenger door and I slid in. He reached over me to grab my seatbelt. I placed my hand on his arm, smiling, and explained, "I can manage on my own."

"Of course you can." He looked disappointed and walked around to the driver's side.

Once we pulled out of the driveway, I asked, "So where are we going?"

He turned to me and adjusted his sunglasses. "Just a quick trip to the desert."

chapter

SEVENTEEN

Lyla

Riley turned down the music in the car. "You are awfully quiet. The whole point of bringing you along was for me to have someone to talk with."

Under my breath, I mumbled, "Or talk to." I hoped he hadn't heard what I said. "Sorry, I was just thinking."

"What are you thinking about?"

"How to get out of this road trip." I paused. Realizing that that was a rude comment, I backtracked. "The desert isn't really my thing."

"That's honest. I promise we'll be home in no time."

"My home? I get to go home?"

"No late night chats with Alex over a smoldering fire and some s'mores? Would you prefer to stay at my house?" Riley lowered his sunglasses and he tried to give me his *come hither* look.

"Do you have an itch? You have a funny expression on your face."

Riley laughed aloud. "God, you are brutal; you're a tiny thing, but you're brutal."

"Why are we going to the desert anyway?"

"I thought I would check on a lead about a group of motorcyclist fanatics and their current interest in an extracurricular activity." Riley turned up the music again.

Flashes of my dream last night began weaving in and out of my head. Everything inside of me screamed for me to get out of the car and run. *Run where?* I thought to myself. At that moment, I decided that I needed to start facing my fears. *Stop being so scared, Lyla. It's exhausting.*

About an hour later, we left the freeway and made a turn onto a narrower highway. Tired of looking at Joshua trees and small clusters of rock formations, I turned to Riley. "Who started the company—I mean this organization—to fight evil?"

"My father did, along with a group of his fellow colleagues."

"Why?"

"Guess the new girl doesn't know the mission statement yet."

"We have a mission statement?"

"Of course. See, this is what a conversation is all about, an exchange of ideas to pass the time and before you know it, voilà. You are at your destination." Riley pulled off the road and onto a dirt road leading to a warehouse, literally in the middle of the desert.

"How did you know this was here?"

"A little bird told me."

"Whatever," I replied, getting out of the car. We started walking to the door.

"So we're just going to have a quick look around and off we go for lunch," said Riley.

"Can we have lunch at the dinosaur place? They have really good apple pies."

"I knew you would be keen on sweets." Riley lifted the heavy-duty lock and chain that was wrapped around the metal handle of the door. He pulled a small black rectangular case from inside his jacket. "So is this restaurant shaped like a dinosaur?" He started to pick the lock.

"No, that would be silly. The gift shop is shaped like a bronto-saurus; the restaurant is shaped like an ordinary restaurant."

"Of course, that's not silly at all." I heard the lock click open.

"Can I sign up to learn how to pick locks too?" Riley had to push hard to get the door to slide open. It squeaked loudly.

"Well, if there is anyone inside, we certainly made our presence known."

"Yes, you did." A man spoke from inside just to the left of the door. He lifted his shotgun and pointed it at Riley's face. It was hard to tell how old the man was. His face had a permanent shade of red from constantly being exposed to the sun. His hair and beard were dark with spots of gray. He wore a yellowing white t-shirt and a leather vest. His jeans were full of dark stains. His bare skin was full of tattoos, almost faded with age.

"Sorry, we must have the wrong warehouse out in the middle of nowhere." Riley reached for my hand and began stepping back.

"No, we've been 'specting you. Come inside." The man cocked his rifle.

"Well, we did drive all the way here. I guess we can stay for a few minutes." Riley walked inside, still holding my hand. I followed closely behind him. "Maybe you should lower your gun. We don't want it accidentally going off." In my head, I could hear Riley say, *"Get ready to run."*

The man began to lower his gun. If I blinked, I would have missed it. Riley grabbed the barrel and shoved the other end into the man's chest. The man let go of the rifle to grab his chest. Riley hit the man again across the face with the butt of the shotgun. The man fell on the ground. I heard footsteps running toward us and started to run for the door.

Then I heard several guns being cocked one after another. When I turned, I saw at least a dozen men, all carrying a weapon of some kind, and they were all aimed at us. Another voice called out from inside the warehouse, "Leaving so soon?" The group of men made way for this man to walk toward us. He took a small handgun from one of the men who had aimed it just a few inches from Riley's head. With the butt of the gun, he hit Riley's head. Riley fell on the ground and a small stream of dark blood began to flow from his temple. I yelled out his name and tried to rush toward him.

A pair of strong arms grabbed my waist. "Oh, no you don't." I could smell sweat, strong body odor, and alcohol from the man who was grabbing too tight and holding me too close to him. He sniffed me. "This one smells nice." The group of men laughed. I wanted to vomit as he licked my ear.

The same man who hit Riley walked over to me. "She's off limits. The buyer was real particular about her not being hurt."

"Oh, come on, Jake. No one gonna need know. I'll be real genteel." This statement resulted in another round of laughter.

Someone I couldn't see chimed in. "What about the guy? Is he off limits too?" The men laughed again.

"That's enough!" Jake was apparently the leader. He was younger than all the other men, bald by choice with tattoos on his neck. He grabbed my wrist, and the man who was holding me quickly let go. He looked at my face and then continued to look me up and down. A wave of panic and fear rushed through me. He pushed me onto another guy, who held my hands behind my back. At least this guy didn't smell as bad. Jake looked at the gun still in his hand. It was already cocked. He pointed it at the man who was holding me before and said, quietly, "You know I hate repeating myself."

"Alright, alright, I got it," the man said with his hands up. "Shit, Jake, I was just joking."

"Put them in the pen. I gotta make a phone call." He turned around and walked away. He stopped by the man who Riley had hit earlier and who was still lying on the floor. Jake kicked him in the side and the man groaned. "Someone take this no-good piece of shit outside. He'll at least make a decent meal for some stupid animal."

Two men grabbed the man's arms and dragged him outside. I could feel a wave of hot air on my back as the door opened. I wanted so badly to run. The man holding my arms twisted my right arm a little harder and I naturally followed him. Another man, the biggest one in the group, grabbed Riley like a sack of flour and put him on his shoulder.

At the corner of the warehouse was a low metal cage. It looked like it was built for animals. The man holding me pushed my head down and shoved me inside the cage. The smell of urine and feces rushed my nostrils and I almost hurled. The cage was definitely used for animals. A small group of men laughed hearing me gag. The big man threw Riley's body in the cage and I heard a thump as Riley hit the floor hard. I rushed to him to check his pulse. It was there, but the blood continued to flow.

The man who shoved me in the cage locked the door. I made eye contact with him. His eyes actually looked a bit sad. "It won't be for long. Jake is already making the phone call to let him know you're here." He didn't wait for me to respond and walked away.

I tended to Riley's wound. I ripped a piece of my undershirt and placed the fabric on his temple to stop the bleeding. The heat was unbearable, and for the first time, I was afraid for my life. I closed my eyes and a picture of the master chef that my father used to work for came into my mind. An old memory soon followed. I was still a little girl and we were in the kitchen. He was cooking noodles. I asked, "Oji-san, how can you cook in this heat?"

He looked up and smiled. "Are you hot? Because I am not. I am standing at the base of Mount Fuji. In fact, snowflakes are falling all around me." He broke his smile and bent to see me closer. "How many times have I asked you to speak Japanese? You are in Japan, and you need to speak Japanese."

"Are you in Japan? Because I am at Disneyland in California. In California, we speak English."

"Clever girl." We both laughed. He handed me a piece of carrot shaped like a flower.

My memory ended when I felt Riley began to stir. He opened his eyes. "Anything happen while I was taking a nap?"

"Yes, I ordered room service, but I ate all of it since you were asleep." Riley tried to sit up but hit his head on the low ceiling of the cage. He moaned from the pain.

"I guess that's karma for bringing you here."

"Why are we here? These people aren't Jay Leno's crew whose hobby is to ride motorcycles on the weekends." In a hushed voice, I added, "They're a bike gang, and they knew we were coming, Riley."

Riley placed his head on my lap, "I know, they were 'specting us." He tried to mimic the man we first encountered.

"It's not funny anymore. I'm really scared."

"I'm sorry," he said, searching his pockets.

"They took our phones away, your wallet, your lock-pick set, and your car is probably being chopped into pieces by now."

"Great," he said taking a deep sigh and squeezing his eyes shut.

I opened my purse and took out two Advil. "Here," I said, placing the pills in his hands.

"I thought—"

"They were kind enough to let me keep my purse...after they took all my money and credit cards."

"That was very generous of them." He popped the pills in his mouth. "You better make it three." I gave him another pill. "Where is everyone?"

"Jake, the leader, said he had to make a phone call to tell whoever it is who wanted us here that we arrived. Our guard is over there in the corner, sleeping." I pointed to the man who carried Riley. He was sleeping on a back seat that was apparently removed from a car. "Another guy comes by once in a while and as far as everyone else..." I shrugged my shoulders. "I don't know—lunch break?" I paused. "We've been set up."

"Indeed." Riley lifted his arm to check the watch that was no longer on his wrist.

"Shit." Riley slapped his wrist.

"Oh, and they took your watch."

"Can't a man get captured and keep his watch?"

"You know what they say, don't wear your Rolex when you meet up with a bike gang."

"No one has ever said that."

"True. I don't really know anyone who owns a Rolex." A few minutes later I asked, "Who's your little birdie?"

"My soon-to-be-dead little birdie is a mole I often use. He's been reliable until now. He said he saw a young boy the last time he was here for a deal. He also said this place was now abandoned. I brought you along to see if you could sense something." He paused and closed his eyes, "I'm sorry, Lyla. I should have been more careful."

"It's okay. I just really don't understand why anyone would want to kill me."

"Think about it, Lyla, you could touch someone and know that they are Pure Evil."

"It doesn't work that way. Besides, isn't there anyone else who can do that already?"

Riley stared at me for a long time and finally replied, "Not yet."

"It's pointless to talk about it now," I said, looking around. We spent the next half an hour in silence. The heat was beginning to get to me; I was starting to feel light-headed and nauseous. I had stopped swatting the flies when they landed on me.

Riley finally opened his eyes. "So, Lyla, since our guts might be ripped out from our stomachs and used as appetizers for the buzzards, I might as well ask you, how come you don't like me? People generally like me, but not you." He swatted a fly that landed on my arm.

"Are you kidding me right now? Besides, I heard there's a buyer coming for me. So you're the only one who gets to be road kill. And anyway, who said I don't like you?"

"Don't you?"

"I don't dislike you." I tried to swallow my saliva, but my mouth had gone dry.

"But you don't like me either?"

I blinked my eyes to clear my head. It wasn't that I didn't like him. I figured I might as well be honest, so I cleared my throat and said, "I don't trust you."

"What?" He tried to get up.

"Don't, you'll hit your head again." He placed his head on my lap and looked at me with steady eyes. "Does my answer bother you?" Riley looked away. "I don't trust you to have the best intentions. And if God gave us these special powers to do good, then I don't really understand you."

"Is everything black and white with you? That's kind of naive isn't it?"

"I'm not naive. I just need things to make sense."

"And I don't make sense?"

We both stopped talking when we heard motorcycles coming closer and closer. Within minutes, we heard voices outside the warehouse. Someone was opening the door.

This is it. I told myself to stop thinking and just rely on my senses.

chapter

EIGHTEEN

Alex

I slammed my cell phone on the dashboard. I was angry with Riley for taking Lyla out of the house. Clearly, he didn't understand how much danger Lyla was in. I had initially felt bad about putting a tracking device on her phone, but now I would have kicked myself if I hadn't done it.

My phone beeped. I hoped it was Simon with Lyla's location. I headed east on the freeway, anticipating that Lyla and Riley headed to the desert. Simon confirmed their direction, and I punched in the last known coordinates on my GPS. Something Simon said at the end of our phone conversation didn't sit well with me. The tracking device on Lyla's cell was heading farther east toward Arizona. I asked Simon to follow the tracking device. I knew Lyla was in danger, but my gut feeling told me she wasn't near her cell phone any more.

I stepped on the gas pedal a little harder at the thought of how scared Lyla was about her dream last night.

Two hours later, I pulled off the highway near the outskirts of the Joshua Tree National Park. I could see a rundown warehouse a quarter of a mile away with two motorcycles parked out front. When I got to the warehouse I got out of the car and walked around back, hoping to find a second entrance.

I found broken windows in the back of the warehouse, but they were too high for me to reach. The only way in was through the front door. I stopped in front of the door to see if I could sense the people inside. There were five or six people inside. I distinctly felt Riley's feeling; he was angry and anxious. This confirmed my gut feeling that they were both in danger. I became furious after I sensed lust from one person. The hunger was strong and raw. By the amount of testosterone I was sensing I could tell he was male. I wanted to kill this person if Lyla was the object of his need to dominate. Two of the people inside were scared, the fear you have when you didn't know what was going to happen.

I knocked, and then I heard footsteps approaching the door. The footsteps were heavy and the man took short breaths. A heavyset man opened the door and demanded, "What do you want?" He used his hand to shield his eyes from the sun, which was shining directly on his face, making it hard to see me.

"I came for the girl."

The man stepped back, and I entered the building. I kept walking toward him, forcing him to walk backwards. Another voice yelled out, "Hey, who is it?"

"A guy, he says he came for the girl."

Another man walked out carrying an assault rifle. He rested the tip of the rifle on his shoulder and scratched his left cheek with his free hand. "Jake didn't say nothing about the girl getting picked up yet."

Playing along, I said, "I don't have all day."

"We can't just give her to you."

"I want to see the girl." I stared him down.

"You don't tell me what to do. Who the fuck do you think you are?" I was about to grab his rifle when he said, "Fine, follow me. I'll take you to her." Riley must have persuaded him.

The heavyset man stepped in front of the guy with the rifle, "What the fuck? Jake is going to be pissed if he finds out we let someone in here."

"You let him in, asshole."

"Fine, but it's your ass on the line, not mine."

The heavyset man stepped aside. The man with the rifle led me deeper into the warehouse. I could see Lyla and Riley held in a locked cage. There was another guy in the corner, but his loud snoring told me he wouldn't be an issue. The stench was overwhelming.

"There, you saw her, now leave." The man with the rifle was sweating. He was probably trying hard to fight Riley's persuasion.

I turned to Riley and pointed to the heavyset guy. "Tell this man to let you out." I turned my attention to the man with the rifle. As quickly as possible, I grabbed the rifle out of the man's hands and hit him on the head with it. He staggered but didn't fall. I turned around to give me momentum and kicked him on the chest. He fell on his back, unconscious. The heavyset guy finished opening the lock to the cage. I walked over and hit him on the back of his head with the butt of the rifle. He fell on the floor and passed out.

I helped Lyla out of the cage, and Riley crawled out after her. "Are you okay?" I asked, scanning her body up and down for any visible wounds.

"Yes," she answered.

"There's one more guy," Riley announced just as a bullet hit the ground a few feet from where we were standing. "As I was saying."

I grabbed Lyla's hand and placed my hand on her head, forcing her to duck low. We hid behind some old metal barrels.

"You stay with Lyla. I'll go around and distract him. Then run out the door. My car is parked outside, north," I whispered to Riley.

Riley winked at Lyla and bolted out in the open. He was never good at following directions. The man started shooting at him. I could see him now. He was standing behind some wooden boxes. His aim was getting closer and closer to Riley.

Lyla looked straight into my eyes. "Go, I promise to stay here."

I believed her but I still needed to say, "Stay right here." I ran in the opposite direction from the way Riley had run and made my way around the warehouse to the shooter's location. He didn't see or hear me approaching him from behind. I kicked the back of his knee and he fell on his knees, dropping the gun. I punched the left side of his stomach three times, and he fell on the floor clutching his side. I picked him up and dragged him to the cage. He was screaming and cursing at me. I stopped, kicked him, and told him to shut up. He did, and then he obediently crawled into the cage. Riley dragged one of the men, still unconscious, toward the cage.

"I'm always cleaning up after you." Riley said as he stuffed the man in the cage.

"Shh," I said putting my hand up. "Where's the snoring guy?" Riley locked the gate as fast as he could, and I ran back to where I had left Lyla. I got there just in time to see another heavyset man crash down on the empty metal barrels face first. Lyla, who had hoisted herself up using the metal chains hanging from the ceiling, jumped down.

"What? I stayed put." I was glad to hear Riley behind me. I don't think I could have stopped myself from running to Lyla and holding her in my arms.

Riley looked at the man on the floor and then at Lyla. "Nice. Now, come on, I'm going to need help with the big guy."

"I thought this *was* the big guy," Lyla replied.

"No, my guy is way bigger," Riley answered back.

"Enough," I said in a stern voice. Some of the liquid spilled from the barrel. I dipped my finger on a small pool of liquid. I smelled my finger. "Gasoline." Turning to Lyla, I said, "Can you stand by the door and let us know if you hear anyone coming?" Riley and I began to pick up the man that Lyla just knocked out. Lyla had just headed for the door when a distant noise that was growing louder pretty quickly stopped us in our tracks. A group of motorcycles was getting closer to the warehouse.

"Uh, Alex, I think I hear someone coming."

Riley and I both dropped the guy on the floor.

chapter

NINETEEN

Lyla

"Time for Plan B," Riley announced.

"Right, Plan B," Alex said. He grabbed my hand and headed toward the back of the building. I had to run to keep up. "There are some broken windows back there."

Once we reached the wall, Riley and Alex both looked up. The windows were too high for us to reach on our own. They immediately began placing barrels and crates up against the wall for us to climb.

"I'll go first," announced Alex. Without waiting for our response, he jumped onto the stacked-up crates and hurled himself up the window's ledge. Kicking the remaining pieces of glass out of the way, he jumped out the window.

"You're up," Riley told me. He climbed up the crates and stopped on the highest crate. "Come on up; you can stand on my shoulders and reach the ledge," he said, patting his shoulders and giving me a smile. I gave him a puzzled look and started to walk back. "It'll be okay, Lyla. Don't be scared," he called out after me.

I took a few more steps to give me enough room to run. Using the momentum from my sprint, I landed on one of the crates with my left foot. With my right foot, I landed on Riley's shoulder, and then I propelled myself onto the window's ledge. The ledge was made out of metal, and it felt hot under my feet. Alex was on the ground waiting. He shouted at me, "I'll catch you, I promise. Now jump." I did. I landed in his arms. For a brief second, he held me tight and close to him. Then he let me go. I heard Riley land next to us.

"We better move it. They are almost inside the warehouse." Riley announced. Sure enough, we heard yelling, and I could make out the F-word used generously. We started running toward Alex's car that was parked a few hundred feet away.

"There they are! I found them," said a voice from above us. I turned around, and a man I didn't recognize was standing at the window we had jumped out of and pointing at us.

"Plan C," Riley yelled out. Alex grabbed something from his pocket and handed it to Riley. Riley started running back toward the warehouse.

"Keep running," Alex yelled out as he grabbed my hand. I turned to see what Riley meant by Plan C. He hurled a small silver metal object onto the window where the man was standing and yelling at us.

"That's for the Rolex, mate!" Riley yelled back.

"Run faster!" Alex demanded. I could hear Riley running hard after us.

I'm not sure how much later it was when I heard a loud explosion and felt a burst of heat on my back that was strong enough to hurl me forward. I landed facedown on the ground. A moment later, I felt Alex's body on top of me. His hand was covering my face. A large piece of sheet metal landed a few inches from our heads. Alex held me tighter underneath him. Pieces of metal and debris continued to fly at us, hitting me on parts of my body that were not sheltered under Alex's body.

I don't know how long we stayed in that position. It felt like time just stopped. We finally got up, but I couldn't hear what Alex was saying, just a loud ringing in my ears. It seemed like he was asking if I was okay. I nodded.

The ringing finally subsided. "What just happened?" I asked, but the only reply I got was a confused look on Alex's face. He continued dialing his cell phone. I heard him give our location and ask a cleaning crew to come as soon as possible.

Riley answered me. "You're safe now." He was patting his clothes down, causing billows of dust to come puffing out. He pulled out a small piece of metal that was lodged in his arm. Blood began to soak his shirtsleeve.

"You were rescued too, Riley." In a small voice I asked, "Oh my God, are all those people dead?" Neither one of the brothers answered me. "Did we just kill all those men?"

Finally Riley spoke up. "That bike gang has a propensity for violence. They don't believe in being civil to human beings."

"Shouldn't we wait to see who was going to pick me up?" I asked, not wanting to check the cause of a growing pain on the back of my heel.

"I doubt they're coming anymore. There wouldn't be a pick-up in the first place if *someone wasn't stupid enough to take you out of the house!*" Alex said, yelling the last few words at Riley's face.

"I wouldn't have done it had I known how much danger she was in. You could have shared some info with me, little bro!" Riley shouted back.

"I thought that was evident when I told you and Father about someone trying to kill her in her apartment." Alex grabbed Riley's shirt.

"Obviously not." Riley shoved Alex.

"Oh, stop it, both of you!" I yelled, causing my throat to feel more parched. "It's both your faults.

"*My* fault?" both brothers replied in unison, turning to face me.

"Yes, your fault," I pointed at Riley. "For being selfish; you brought me here to use me." I mimicked his voice, "'Just wanted to see if you could feel anything.' And you—" I shoved Alex with both my hands. "You with your whispering in my ear that everything is going to be okay. Well, it's not okay!" I shoved him hard. "My dreams are not safe." Alex gave me surprised look. "My gut feeling told me not to come out here, but all I heard was your voice in my head telling me that I was safe, that everything would be okay." I shoved him again. "So please, stop telling me I'll be safe and that I'm not alone. And for crying out loud, why did you park so far away?"

With his head down, Alex answered, "I didn't want them to see me coming."

"Liar, you didn't want to risk damaging your car," Riley countered.

"Well, that too."

I started walking toward Alex's car, not bothering to see if they were following me. I felt a wave of pain every time I stepped on my right heel and tried to place my weight on my toes.

"Are you okay?" Alex asked, quickly catching up to me.

"I'm okay, except for the ringing in my ears."

"It'll go away," Alex explained.

"Let's go home," I said.

"Wait." He gently gripped my shoulder. I stopped, and Alex knelt on one knee and lifted my foot. He checked the back of my foot and pulled a small piece of metal out of my shoe. I felt warm blood gushing out and watched as it stained the sand around my foot. Without asking, he put my arm around his neck and lifted me in his arms. He started walking again while carrying me.

"I can walk on my own." He didn't say anything. I avoided making eye contact with him. "This is a bit awkward," I said quietly.

"Tell me about it," Riley answered for Alex again.

"You are surprisingly heavier than you look," Alex finally said after a few minutes of walking.

"Bet you wish you didn't park so far away now?" We walked the rest of the way to Alex's car in silence.

The air from the AC in the car felt good on my skin, which was now covered in dirt, dust, and grime. From the back, I could see Alex's reflection in the rearview mirror. He looked up and caught me staring. I quickly turned my head and focused on the Joshua trees outside my window. Neither Alex nor Riley spoke for the remainder of our car ride. I closed my eyes and fell asleep.

It was already dark by the time I woke up. There was a bottle of water near me that hadn't been there when I fell asleep. My shoe was on the floor of the car. The wound on my heel had stopped bleeding and it was bandaged up. "Can I drink this?" I asked.

"Yes, but slowly," Alex answered me.

I looked around and realized that we had arrived in the city. We were not on the freeway that led to my house. "Guess I'm still not going home?" I already knew the answer.

Riley turned his head to face me. "You can always stay with me." I didn't reply and closed my eyes again.

We pulled up to Alex's driveway. We all got out of the car. Alex threw the car keys to Riley. "You roomies have fun now," Riley said as he caught the car keys. He slipped into the driver's seat and rolled down the window. "Lyla, I'm sorry. I wouldn't intentionally put you in harm's way. I hope you know that."

"It's okay, I needed to get some sun anyway," I replied, not completely sure what I was supposed to say to a man who just delivered me to my kidnappers.

It felt strange to follow Alex into his house. Once inside, Alex turned to me, "The doctor should be here soon."

"I don't need a doctor," I protested.

"He's on his way. Don't leave…"

I finished his sentence for him, "I know, don't leave the house or open the door." Alex gave me a steady look and then left me alone in his massive living room. I watched as he quickly made his way up the stairs.

I tried to make my way up, careful not to put my weight on my heel. It was difficult since the stairs did not have any railing for me to hold onto. I didn't hear Alex make his way back to me until he was on the stair above me. "Sorry, I forgot." He lifted me again and carried me up the stairs. "I know, awkward," he said, and I gave a small laugh. Once inside my room, he placed me on the bed. I sat up. "You probably have time to take a shower before the doctor gets here."

"A shower sounds good."

"I'll, uh…" Alex looked uncomfortable.

"I can manage on my own."

"I'll leave you to it, then." He walked toward the door then turned back to face me, "Evans, I never meant to hurt you in any way."

I stared at a spot on the floor. "I know; I didn't mean what I said."

"But you were right." He walked out.

A wave of regret rushed though me at the thought that he might never hold me again. My dreams had always made me feel like a coward. I had come to like not feeling scared during my dreams. Alex had helped me face something that I had always hidden and retreated from. I knew the distance between us just become as wide as the ocean.

chapter

TWENTY

Lyla

I wiped away a tear that was quickly gaining momentum down my cheek. I knew more would come if I didn't get up at that moment. I took a shower, and as soon as I put on a pair of jeans and a shirt, there was a knock on my door. I opened the door and saw Alex in a simple white t-shirt and pajama bottoms. He looked different. I have to admit, I liked seeing him this way.

"Dr. Jenskee is waiting downstairs. There's food in the fridge. I'm gonna go to bed, but let me know if you need anything." Without waiting for me to answer he walked toward his room.

I apologized to the doctor for making him come out in the middle of the night. He was nice enough to make me feel less guilty. He checked for bruises and broken bones and eventually concluded that I was fine but told me to take it easy for a few days and to drink plenty of water. He confirmed that the ringing in my ears from the blast would go away in a day or so, and he spread antibiotic cream on my cuts. He cleaned the wound on my heel and told me it was a minor cut that should heal nicely.

"Did you get a chance to check Alex?" I asked. Dr. Jenskee looked up. He was putting his belongings bag in his bag.

"Is he hurt?"

"He made himself my human shield."

"I see." He opened a medicine bottle and gave me two pills. "Take these. They will help with the aches and pains." I nodded. "Take them after you've had something to eat."

"Okay," I replied.

"I'll go check on Alex." Dr. Jenskee looked up toward the second floor of the house and said, "I hate those stairs."

"Me too." We both laughed.

Dr. Jenskee made his way up the stairs and I headed to the kitchen. I opened the fridge and found lots of food, but I wasn't hungry. I grabbed a water bottle and headed back to my room.

The silence in the house was getting to me. Once in my room, I turned the television on. I flipped through the channels and caught the last ten minutes of *Fashion Police*. *Keeping Up With the Kardashians* was next, but I couldn't bring myself to watch it. The relationships among the siblings on that show have always fascinated me. Maybe because I didn't have any brothers or sisters. Whenever I started watching the show, David, Beck, Lance, and especially my father would walk right out of the room. Although Lance sometimes stayed just long enough to check out Kim.

I settled in to watch the news, realizing that it had been a few days since I had felt a part of the real world. There was a report on a car chase that ended with the driver being caught and then opening fire at the police officers with an assault rifle. This scene hit too close to home given all the guns I had seen today.

Feeling overwhelmed, I turned the television off. It was too much for me to accept that people would intentionally hurt others. I closed my eyes, and flashes of the day's events came flooding in. I shuddered, remembering the horrible man who had held me too close to him and his disgusting breath on my neck. I ran to the bathroom and vomited.

There on the bathroom floor, I curled up in a ball and cried. I wanted my dad so much it hurt. I could feel my heart aching. My chest felt like it was closing in. I wanted my friends near me. They had always helped distract me from being emotional, from accepting the truth about me. Then I finally began forming the thought I had avoided for years. There would come a time when they would move on. They would have families of their own and I would be alone.

I closed my eyes and saw the girl from my first grade class. I was waiting in line at the drinking fountain. She pulled on my hair and teased, "Guess what I know," a smirk on her face.

"What?" I asked innocently.

"That you don't have a mom."

"I do too have a mom."

"Liar. My mom is friends with the office lady, and she said your mom left you."

"She didn't leave me." I bit my bottom lip to keep from crying.

"You think you're so pretty, Lyla, but you're not. Even your mom didn't think you were pretty. She couldn't stand looking at your ugly face and she left you."

I just stood there and cried. The boy who was in front of me in line had just finished drinking from the fountain. He turned to me and said, "It's your turn." I just looked at him. He insisted, "It's okay, I'll wait for you. Then we can play on the jungle gym."

"Why?" I asked him.

"Cause I think you're the prettiest girl I've ever met." David and I have been friends ever since.

At some point, I ran out of tears. I was too tired to continue pitying myself. I had two truths to accept. First, my dad wasn't around to help me anymore. Second, I had become too selfish expecting David to continue rescuing me.

116

It's time to move on, I told myself. First, I needed to stop playing the victim. *Get up, now!* I washed my face and walked over to the desk. I found my notebook in the first drawer. I figured there must be some tape somewhere in this house. I started writing down every fact I could think of that I'd learned since starting work at the company. I was determined to find out who was trying to kill me and why. One thing I was sure about was that whoever wanted me killed was connected to the company and to the murders I was researching. It was too much to be a mere coincidence.

Sunlight was beginning to stream through my windows when I posted the last piece of paper on the wall. I stepped back and looked at the wall opposite of the bed that was now filled with papers posted with facts in chronologic order. The answer I was looking for was on this wall. I just needed to figure it out.

chapter

TWENTY ONE

Alex

I prayed to God that I would do anything if he would just make Lyla stop crying. It occurred to me that I hadn't said one prayer since I asked Him to bring my mother back. I was eight years old then. I felt as helpless then as I did now. He didn't answer my prayers then.

Even twenty feet away from her room, my heart ached as I felt every inch of Lyla's pain and sadness. No wonder she hid them behind walls. It was too much to bear. I could also feel a similar feeling, a feeling of abandonment. Someone she loved very much had abandoned her. I yearned to reach out to her and to tell her I understood what she was feeling.

I was glad to get Riley's call. Simon's team had caught up to the bikers who had Lyla's cell phone. They were being interrogated at one of our more discreet locations. I called the other two men on the team, who were watching the house, to let them know that I was leaving. Then I called Flora and asked her to come to the house; I told her I would wait until she arrived.

I stopped outside the door to Lyla's room before I left. I couldn't hear anything, but I could still feel her overwhelming sense of sadness. It seemed to stem from an old memory. She was remembering something that had hurt her a long time ago. I left the house as quickly as I could. Her pain was overwhelming me.

Once inside the building, I was met by Lupe. "Sorry, Alex, Riley didn't want to wait anymore. He is in the interrogation room with a man who refers to himself as Jake. He seems to be the leader of the bike gang."

I watched the interrogation through the one-way mirror. Lupe walked in after me with two cups of coffee, handing me one and keeping one for herself. "Thanks," I said. She gave me a surprised look. "What, don't I always say 'thank you'?" Lupe laughed in response.

Inside the interrogation room, Riley handed Jake a cigarette. "I know you're just trying to make a buck," he said. He reached over the table and lit the cigarette. Jake puffed his cigarette without breaking his stare from Riley. He lifted both hands to take the cigarette out of his mouth; his wrists were tied with a plastic tie.

"So tell me how you know about Lyla." Jake inhaled a long and deep drag from his cigarette. Riley looked up toward us. That was his sign to Lupe that he needed a little boost to persuade Jake to tell us what we wanted to know.

Jake exhaled a steady puff of smoke. "This man calls me up a few days ago. Said he had a job for us. He said his daughter was out of hand and she was running with the wrong crowd and dating a guy he didn't approve of." He pointed to Riley, "I guess that's you. The man said he was going to make it so that his daughter and you will go to the warehouse out in the desert. All we had to do was detain you guys until he got there. He promised to pay us twenty grand.

Sounded pretty easy to me, almost like we were doing a service, you know. I wouldn't want his lovely daughter dating the wrong guy."

"Twenty grand just to babysit," Riley responded.

Jake looked down at his hands, "There was talk of permanently putting you down for a nap, if needed."

"Have you ever seen or met this man?" Riley placed his arms behind his head and leaned back in his chair.

"No, there was just that one phone call and a text with the picture of your girl." It annoyed me that Jake referred to Lyla as Riley's girl.

"So you just trusted him?" Riley asked as Jake dropped his ashes on the floor.

"I figured there was nothing to lose." Jake took another hit of his cigarette. "Just needed a couple of guys to be at the warehouse to wait for you."

"The man said he was going to meet you at the warehouse. Why were you heading east?"

"I'm a businessman. I figured if he was willing to pay twenty grand, then maybe he'd be willing to pay double. I told him to meet me at the coffee shop right before the Arizona border and to bring the money."

"And if he didn't?"

"Then we deliver his daughter one piece at a time until he paid." There was no remorse in this statement.

"So what happened at the coffee shop?"

"I don't know, man. No one came, and the next thing I know your men grabbed us." Jake dropped his cigarette butt on the floor and smashed it with the heel of his boot.

Riley leaned in. "Is there anything else you want to tell me?" Lupe placed her hands on both sides of her temple.

"That's all I know, I swear."

Lupe gave me a nod.

Riley leaned in and asked, "Do you have any outstanding warrants?"

"Uh…" Beads of sweat were running down Jake's forehead. I could tell that he was trying hard not to answer this question. "Yeah, man."

"What are they for?"

"Assault with a deadly weapon in Texas and—does Mexico count?"

"Yes."

"Manslaughter," Jake sighed.

"Good, you've done well. One last question: do you know what happened to my watch?"

"Your what? I don't know what the fuck happened to your stupid watch."

"All right, all right, no need to be nasty. You will never want to do anything illegal for the rest of your life." Jake's pupils became enlarged.

"Yeah, you got it," Jake replied. Two of our men came in and dragged Jake away. Our chief of security walked in. "A warrant for manslaughter in Mexico and a warrant for assault in Texas," Riley explained.

"We'll take care of it, Mr. St. James."

Riley walked out of the interrogation room and joined Lupe and me. "Thanks, Lupe."

"Any time, as long as it's not Lyla," Lupe answered back.

"That hard?" Riley asked.

"It took every ounce of strength I had to calm her down enough to stay in that room. She wanted to bolt."

"I don't blame her. So what do you think?" Riley asked me.

"Whoever it is, he knows too much about Lyla," I answered.

"And us," Riley added. I looked at Riley. "He used my mole to get to me and knew I would take Lyla out to that warehouse."

"Or she knew?" Lupe chimed in.

"Dammit, it could be anyone." I slammed my fist on the table.

chapter

TWENTY TWO

Lyla

It was early afternoon when I finally woke up and got dressed. I had fallen asleep without changing or even getting under the covers. I went downstairs, but no one was there to greet me—just more food in the kitchen. I made myself a cup of coffee, and I couldn't hear any noise anywhere in the house except for the sounds I was making. I decided to go up and knock on Alex's door. No one answered. When I came downstairs, the same man who had stopped me from going out yesterday morning was waiting by the door.

"Good Morning, Ms. Evans. I'll be taking you to work this morning. Are you ready?"

"Yes...I'm sorry, I didn't catch your name."

"Adam."

"Lyla, nice to meet you."

Adam dropped me off at the front of the building. I walked in the lobby; Lupe was waiting for me. "Morning, girl. Your eye bag looks worse than mine."

"The last twenty-four hours has been a bit rough," I said, following Lupe to the elevator. The elevator went down instead of up.

"I heard about your adventure in the desert. What was it like being rescued by the two brothers?"

"Technically, only one brother did the saving." Lupe laughed and placed a cell phone that looked identical to mine in my hand.

"I heard that too. Typical Riley. You have to tell me all about it. You have training this afternoon. Lucky—I wish I was working out instead of being stuck behind a desk."

"Lucky—I wish I was stuck behind a desk instead of working out." We both giggled. It felt nice to laugh.

Lupe led me to the changing room and pointed out a locker that was designated for me. "I gotta run, but your password is"—she raised her arm and looked at the back of her hand—"3356." We both laughed again. "I'm not very good at remembering numbers."

"I'm not very good at keeping myself from getting kidnapped," I answered. We shared another round of laughter.

"My stomach is starting to hurt from all this laughing. I really gotta go. Have a good workout." Lupe gave me a hug and left me alone in the locker room. I checked and replied to the texts on my phone. There were a couple from David and Beck. It was odd not to hear from Lance.

In the locker, I found workout clothes and running shoes in my size. I quickly changed and walked back out to the hallway. Simon was in his gym clothes waiting for me.

"Simon!" I gave him a smile.

"Hey, Lyla—ready to work out?"

"How come you weren't at the house this morning?"

"Mr. St. James wanted to change things up a bit."

"I see."

"He also said that you were pretty good at defending yourself, but he wanted me to show you a few moves just in case."

"Just in case I get kidnapped again." I laughed a little, but Simon didn't.

"I'm sorry about that. I should have been there at the house."

"It's okay, you probably had other damsels in distress to protect."

"It was my day off. Sorry."

"It's not your fault, Simon. Now come on, show me these moves."

It was nice to let my aggression out. Simon was a good coach, and he taught me some boxing moves. He was patient with me and broke down the moves until I got the hang of them. He encouraged me to be more aggressive and not wait until my opponent was attacking me, saying that even though I small, I was fast and I should use it to my advantage. I smiled remembering a childhood friend who gave me the same advice.

After showering and changing out of my workout clothes, I walked out of the locker room and found Alex leaning against the wall with his arms crossed and his head down. He was wearing a very nice fitted suit. Just when I thought he couldn't look anymore handsome, he goes and puts on a suit.

"Got a hot date?" I asked jokingly.

"Finally—let's go. Father wants you to have dinner with us." He spoke as he began walking away. He walked with long strides. I had to jog a few steps to catch up.

"Wait, what do you mean your father wants me to have dinner you?"

He stopped and turned around to look at me, but he was glaring. I think I was annoying him with my questions. "What part don't you understand?"

I had to quickly stop myself from bumping into him. "The part about your father and dinner? Is everyone going?"

"The entire company can't fit around my grandmother's dining table."

"Was that sarcasm? Sorry, I almost missed it. I was too busy deciphering what your glares meant. Do they mean *stop annoying me with*

your silly questions or *you better take me seriously, I'm not just a pretty face?"*
Alex didn't say anything. I felt guilty about talking to him in such
a saucy manner. "Wait, I'm going to your grandmother's house?" I
looked down at my jeans and worn-out ballet flats. "Should I change?"

"Amanda picked out some dresses out for you."

I let out a deep sigh.

"What?" Alex demanded.

"Nothing," I replied.

"For goodness sake, just say it."

"I can dress myself."

Alex didn't reply and continued walking down the hallway. He
didn't say much in the car either. We drove north on the 5 freeway,
eventually pulling into the private airport in Burbank. He parked
the car in a private hangar near a white jet. The stairs of the airplane
were down and a man dressed in a pilot uniform nodded to us. I
finally asked him, "Are we getting on that plane?"

"Yes, now please get out of the car, Evans. We're late."

"Where are we going?"

"I already told you, my grandmother's house."

"Where does your grandmother live?"

"San Francisco."

I followed Alex up the small flight of stairs into the plane. I
had never been in a private jet before. Riley was sitting in one of the
chairs sipping a glass of a dark, brownish gold liquid. "Not like you
to be late for grandma's dinner, little brother," Riley commented as
we boarded. He wasn't alone. A blond woman with long legs dressed
in a tight blue dress sitting next to him laughed at his comment.
Even her laughter was sexy. Riley was wearing a dark silver suit,
perfectly tailored like all of his suits.

I was feeling even more under-dressed. I waved my hand in
their direction, and Riley gestured to one of the chairs opposite theirs.
The woman didn't even look my way and busied herself with a drink.
I noticed her eyes scoping out Alex. I think she was comparing the
two of them to determine if she was with the better-looking sibling.

Riley offered me a drink. I just asked for water and peanuts—my poor attempt to lighten the mood. Riley laughed but once again; I could never really tell if it was genuine or not. I heard a deep sigh from Alex, which I was beginning to notice meant he was annoyed.

"I wouldn't have guessed you would bring Lyla as your date." Riley stared intently at his drink, avoiding Alex's glare.

"She's not my date. I have strict orders to protect her, so I couldn't just leave her now, could I?" Alex answered abruptly.

"What, I wasn't invited? Alex, wait. I don't want to go somewhere that I'm not invited. I could have just stayed at your house. I would have promised not to go anywhere. Or I could have stayed with one of—"

Alex finished my sentence for me. "Your friends? Do you really think they can protect you?"

Before I could reply, the door to the cockpit opened and the pilot came out. It wasn't the same man who greeted us outside the plane.

"Good evening, my name is Benjamin Clark and I'll be flying you to San Francisco tonight. If we aren't waiting on anyone else, I will go ahead and close the cabin doors."

"Go ahead, Mr. Clark. We are all present and accounted for," Riley replied.

As the pilot closed the door, I didn't realize that I was staring at him until he said my name. "Lyla, it's me, Ben."

"Ben! I thought that was you." I cried out and jumped out of my seat to hug him.

"How are you?" he asked.

"I'm fine, and you're a pilot—just what you said you would do. That's great," I said to him.

Alex cleared his throat. "We're on a tight schedule, Ben." Alex said his name with such disdain. I knew he wasn't very patient, but that was the first time I had witnessed him being obnoxious.

"Yes, of course, we'll be taking off now, sir."

I mouthed the words, "I'm sorry."

As soon as we were in the air, Riley and his friend started getting to know each other intimately. I was glad that the chair swiveled completely around so that I didn't have to watch them make out all the way to San Francisco.

The cockpit door opened again and Ben came out. "I just wanted to make sure you guys were okay and if you needed anything."

I looked past Ben and stared at all the gadgets in the cockpit. "Can I go in there?"

"Sure," Ben replied with a big, warm smile.

I unbuckled my seatbelt and followed him. Ben sat down on his chair and told me to sit in a small black chair directly behind his chair. He introduced me to the other pilot, the one who had greeted us outside the plane. He was older and very nice. Ben pointed out the major controls and explained what they did. The other pilot shared a few of Ben's embarrassing stories from when he first started flying.

Ben and Lani, my suitemate in college, had dated each other starting in our freshman year. For spring break senior year, Ben and Lani went to Hawaii to visit Lani's family. On the second day of spring break, I got a call from them asking me to fly out to Hawaii. They were married two days later.

Ben announced that he and Lani were expecting their first child. I squealed. Ben explained that Lani had sent me a message via Facebook, and I explained that it had been a while since I'd checked my Facebook page. The other pilot added that Ben already bought a baby pilot uniform. Ben turned red and we all laughed.

We all stopped laughing when Alex walked in and grabbed my arm. "She should probably sit back down in her chair and buckle up for our descent."

"Yes, of course," the older pilot answered.

When I got my seatbelt on, I asked Alex, "What was that about? I wasn't bothering them."

"I'm supposed to be protecting you. I can't very well do that if the plane crashes."

"Ben has wanted to be pilot since he was a little boy. He would never not take his job seriously."

"And how do you know that?"

"He's an old friend."

"Great, another friend. How have you managed to have so many friends?" I wasn't sure where the conversation was going, but I resented the way he said the word *friends*.

"At least I have friends," I mumbled.

"That's the problem, Evans. You have too many friends," Alex replied quickly.

I didn't want to continue this conversation anymore. I've heard it too many times in past relationships, or I should say, failed relationships. I didn't feel like I needed to explain myself to Alex.

When the plane landed, I said goodbye to Ben and promised to contact him and Lani soon. I didn't bother explaining who Lani was to Alex.

There were two cars waiting for us. Riley descended the flight of stairs first, with his date following closely behind. "See you at dinner, and do try to hurry. You know how Grandma hates to wait." Riley and his date climbed into the backseat of one of the cars. Alex directed me to the other car. I got in, but Alex stopped to speak to the driver before getting into the car.

On the drive, we didn't speak one word to each other. We headed toward downtown San Francisco. The car pulled over at one of the streets lined with high-end clothing stores. Alex got out and motioned for me to get out as well, saying, "You have ten minutes."

"For what?" I asked getting out of the car.

"To pick out your own dress," he replied in a monotone voice.

"Oh." I wasn't sure what he was trying to tell me so I just stared at him.

"In nine minutes and thirty seconds, I'm going to instruct the driver to take us to my grandmother's house in whatever you are wearing."

"Oh!" I said with more emphasis, and I rushed into the Calvin Klein store, figuring I could find a decent dress that my credit card could handle. I zeroed in on a coral dress with a belt. The saleslady immediately helped me into one of the fitting rooms. The dress fit, and I gathered my clothes and slipped my shoes back on. I checked my watch and saw that I still had about five minutes left to run next door and look for any shoes that would be more suitable than my well-worn black ballet flats. I told the saleslady that I would wear the dress out, and she helped me cut off the tag and gave me a bag to put my old clothes in. I hastened to the cashier, and the man behind the counter explained that my friend had already paid for it. *I'll just pay him back*, I thought, trying to hurry out of the store.

I didn't notice Alex standing by the door until I bumped into him. My head hit his chest. "Ouch that hurts. Seriously, a little fat wouldn't kill you," I said, rubbing my forehead. He pulled out a black pair of strappy heels from a shoebox.

"Cute, you chose those yourself?"

"Kind off." He bent down on one knee and lifted my left foot.

I saw red on the bottom of the shoes and asked, "Oh my God, are these Christian Louboutins?"

He slipped off my shoe and replaced it with the shoe he'd just bought. I could hear the woman who helped me and several others in the store sigh and make that "aww" sound. I even heard someone say, "It's just like *Pretty Woman*."

"Great, they think I'm a prostitute," I whispered in Alex's ear. He laughed, but I don't think he's ever seen *Pretty Woman* and my joke was once again lost on him. *But at least he laughed,* I thought to myself and that's when I found myself thinking that I could spend the rest of my life doing anything just to hear that laugh. *Oh, shit. I think I'm in trouble. I'm seriously falling for this guy who is technically still my boss, and I can't afford these shoes.*

chapter

TWENTY THREE

Alex

Lyla and I waited outside my grandmother's door. I stole a look. Lyla had chosen a pretty dress. It made her look more feminine and delicate. "You clean up nice, Evans."

"Not too bad yourself, St. James," Lyla responded without looking at me.

The door finally opened and my grandmother stood on the other side of the door with her arms wide open. "You must be, Lyla." She leaned in to hug Lyla, who hid her surprise and returned my grandmother's embrace.

I introduced them to each other, "Evans, this is my grand-mother, Rose St. James. Grandma, this is Ev—Lyla."

"Ms. St. James, it's nice to meet you. I apologize for intruding in your family dinner."

My grandmother pulled Lyla's arm into hers, "Nonsense, child. I explicitly told Nico's father to invite you."

"Nico?" I was hoping Lyla wouldn't catch that.

Grandmother patted me on my arm, "Shame on you for not telling her your full name."

Lyla looked at me, waiting. I sighed, "Alexander Nicholas St. James."

"You'll have to forgive my Nico. He takes after his bitter old grandfather. His name was Nicholas, too. God rest his soul."

"He is a bit like an old man," Lyla agreed, and the two women quietly laughed at my expense.

I cleared my throat. "Maybe we should join the others."

Still laughing, my grandmother agreed and we walked into the parlor. My father, Aunt Marsha, Riley, and his date were sitting and sipping their sherry. Sherry is my grandmother's signature drink before dinner.

My father rose when he saw us. He walked over to Lyla. "Ms. Evans, finally we meet." He shook Lyla's hands. "It is a pleasure to meet you."

"Indeed, we have been most impressed by your gifts," Aunt Marsha added. Aunt Marsha gave Lyla a hug.

"Let's eat," my grandmother announced. "I can hear the chef, and he is ready to serve our first course."

Over dinner, my grandmother tried her best to be fair in shar-ing embarrassing stories of both Riley and myself. She also put a lot of effort into making Riley's date and Lyla as comfortable as possible. Aunt Marsha talked about her new grandchild. My father stayed quiet as usual. Riley made up for the silence that both Father and I contributed. Riley's date passed on dessert, and Lyla's face lit up at the sight of homemade flan.

After dinner, I noticed that Lyla was looking at the framed photos that were scattered all over my grandmother's home. I realized that most of them were of me as a young boy, and I tried to distract her from looking at any more embarrassing pictures of me, but my grandmother was at her side before I could reach her. "This is a photo of the two boys and their mother."

"She's beautiful."

"Yes, she was."

"Was..." Lyla responded in a small voice.

"Yes," my grandmother said, patting Lyla's hand.

I stepped in before Grandmother could respond further. "Evans, we should probably get going. It's getting late."

Ignoring me, Lyla picked up another photo on top of the fireplace. "Nice hat."

"I'll let Riley explain that one."

Riley joined us. "What? I think I look rather dashing in my school uniform. It was a prestigious school, you know." Riley put his hand on the lapel of his suit and in a thick English accent, he mimicked his old headmaster: "It's an honor to be a part of all the tradition Manchester Academy has to offer."

"You went to school in Europe?" Lyla asked.

"Not just a school, my dear girl, but a college preparatory school for lifelong cynics," Riley replied, maintaining his accent.

Lyla laughed. "And you?" she asked, turning to me.

"Down the street for grade school and private tutors until college," I replied.

"I see."

Riley's date joined us. "I'm bored. You promised this would be fun."

"It will be, sweetheart. I always deliver on my promise," Riley replied maintaining his accent. His date laughed. Riley took her hand and announced their departure. Riley gave Grandmother a hug. She whispered something in Riley's ear and held his face for a brief moment. Riley smiled and gave her a kiss on her cheek, then he turned to us, said, "See you both in LA," and they walked out.

I figured this was a good time for Lyla and me to make our exit as well. I walked over to my father and we shook hands. "I'll give your aunt a ride home and stay at a hotel tonight. I have some business to attend to in the morning." Aunt Marsha has a house in Marine County. She spends most of her time here in San Francisco, only flying to Los Angeles for meetings.

I walked over to my aunt, who just finished saying goodbye to Lyla. "Good night, Aunt Marsha."

"Take care of yourself and of this young lady. She's special."

"I know," I replied in a low voice.

It was my grandmother's turn to say goodbye to us. "I already miss you, Nico." She hugged me. Then she turned to Lyla and said, "You are in good hands with my Nico. He won't let anything happen to you. I can't wait to see you again at the gala."

"The gala?" Lyla asked.

"Nico, you will bring her, won't you?"

"Of course, Grandma." They embraced for a long time.

It was cold outside. I realized that Lyla didn't have a coat. I took off my jacket and wrapped it around her shoulders. She protested, but I pretended to be distracted by the fact that our car had just pulled up. The driver stepped out of the car and walked over to open the door for us. "That's okay," I told him, and opened the door for Lyla.

Once inside, Lyla asked me, "Are we flying home as well?"

"No, I thought we could just drive home."

"Just to change things up." She caught on that I was making decisions on a whim.

"Exactly," I smiled.

"Your grandmother is really sweet. Thank you for bringing me to meet her." Lyla covered her mouth with her hand to hide a yawn.

An hour later, Lyla fell asleep. I placed her head on my shoulder. I was glad that we had at least seven more hours to be close to each other.

chapter

TWENTY
FOUR

Alex

I gripped the steering wheel of my car and clenched my teeth. I was furious. How could those two be so stupid as to go to a club? Lyla was insistent that she meet her friends tonight. I was firm in my answer. I explained to her that absolutely no unnecessary risks should be taken. I thought she understood. I should have known she was stubborn and would ask Riley to sneak her out of the house. I pounded on the steering wheel. Riley should have known better. We were still cleaning up the mess from the warehouse incident.

I pulled up in front of the club and gave my keys to a valet. He gave me a white ticket, which I quickly pocketed. I briefly looked over a group of girls who were standing in the front of the line try-ing to get my attention with their assets. I slipped the bouncer a hundred-dollar bill, and he let me in the club. It wasn't the kind of place I would ever visit on my own. The music was too loud.

I quickly found my brother in a booth, a swarm of girls already surrounding him. I walked over, mentally restraining myself from hitting some sense into him.

"There you are! Girls, this is my younger brother. I told you he would come," Riley announced to the girls sitting around him. The girls looked me up and down. Their smiles were too big for my taste.

"This is the stupidest thing you have ever done," I told Riley with my jaw clenched.

"I know you're mad. She would have come even if I hadn't taken her. Relax; she's safe. I've been keeping an eye on her all night."

"Sure, you have," I replied, glancing at the redhead who had her hand on his thigh.

Riley made a signal with his fingers that he had a visual on Lyla. She was at the bar. "Besides, I got some information on our girl."

"What kind of information?"

"For starters, Lyla is very comfortable here. She didn't stand in line and walked straight to the bouncer. He gave her a hug and even opened the door for her. She didn't even glance at all the girls waiting in line who threw her evil looks. You know how petty girls can be."

"Get to the point," I demanded.

"All right, all right. All I'm trying to say is that she's a regular here and she definitely knows the bartender. I saw the way he looked at her. His head shot up as soon as she walked in. She went straight to the bar, and he already had a drink ready for her by the time she sat down on a stool."

"How is any of this relevant?"

"Lyla's a party girl. She's smart and reserved but quite possibly a freak in bed," Riley replied, smiling. "I think I'm in love." Riley took a sip of his drink.

"You're absurd," I retorted. I walked away and found a spot in the back of the club where I had a better view of Lyla, who was still standing at the bar. I made a mental note that her dress was too short and she couldn't possibly run in those heels. The bartender was too eager to please her, and he took every opportunity to show off. Whatever he was saying couldn't be that funny, but she was laughing with him. He placed another drink next to her empty glass.

The bartender kept taking every opportunity to touch her, moving a strand of her hair from her eyes and placing it behind her ears. He was leaning in too close to talk to her. She wasn't doing anything to dissuade him. I'd seen other guys, including my brother, try to flirt with her, and she had always been oblivious to their advances. What was it with this guy? She was actually touching his hand. *Is she flirting back? Damn, I think she was.*

The bartender wasn't even paying attention to the other customers who were standing around the bar waiting impatiently for their drinks. The other bartenders were covering for him. He pulled out his cell phone to answer a call. She downed her drink while waiting for him to finish his conversation. He put his phone away and took two shot glasses from the top shelf. His shirt went up, exposing his stomach, and she didn't look away. Clearly, she was checking him out. He poured clear liquid from a bottle, took her hand, and licked the soft tissue between her thumb and index finger. *Shit, I can't believe she really let him lick her?* He did the same on his hand while she poured salt on her hand and his. He raised his shot glass and she raised hers to meet his. They both downed their drinks and I hated the way he looked at Lyla as she sucked on a wedge of lime. After setting his glass down, he went around the bar and took her by the hand. He led her off to one of the doors on the side.

I was halfway across the dance floor when I couldn't see them anymore, but I noted the door that had just closed. A woman in a short, tacky dress that revealed too much started dancing in front of me, rubbing against my leg. Normally, I would at least be amused, but right now, I needed to get to Lyla. I gently pushed the woman away.

I finally got to the door and pushed through to the staircase on the other side. The bartender was already at the top of the stairs, with Lyla following closely behind him. I ran up the stairs, taking two steps at a time, and grabbed Lyla's hand. She turned around and looked surprised to see me. "Alex, what—?"

"Let's go home, Evans, before you embarrass yourself." I regretted it as soon as it came out.

"Excuse me." She shook her hand free from my grasp.

"Lyla, do you know this guy?" The bartender asked, taking a step toward me.

The door at the top of the stairs opened. It was dark, and then a small cluster of lights came closer to the doorway. Several people jumped out at once and yelled, "Happy birthday, Lyla!" *Dammit, it's her birthday.*

Lyla gave me a dirty look. She walked up the remaining stairs and entered the room. "Aww, you guys. A surprise party? Really?"

The bartender gave me a little shove. "This party is by invitation only, and it doesn't look like you're invited."

"It's okay. He's with me, unfortunately," Lyla said, touching the bartender on his arm.

"You sure?" he asked.

"Yeah," Lyla replied, and the bartender stormed down the stairs.

A man dressed in a deep blue suit and black t-shirt stepped out of the crowd and pulled Lyla into the room. "I know you don't like surprises, but we did it anyways. Happy birthday, Lyla." He walked up to her and kissed her on the cheek. Another guy, wearing glasses and a printed t-shirt with a dinosaur that said, "not fair, I was here first," walked up to her and gave her a hug.

The crowd parted and another guy walked toward Lyla holding the cake. "You gotta blow out the candles before the place burns down," he said, and then he started singing "Happy Birthday" and the rest joined in. After the song was over, the man with the cake told Lyla to make a wish. She closed her eyes briefly and blew her candles. Someone took the cake away. Lyla gave the guy a long hug—too long and too tight. He let go, but not before giving her a peck on the forehead and whispering in her ear. These must be the friends she kept referring to. I recognized their faces from Lyla's file.

An attractive Asian woman with long black hair walked up to Lyla and, in a loud voice, asked, "Lyla, you brought a guest?" Everyone turned to me.

"Oh, right, this is Alex from work." She looked at me. "I work with him, my boss...Alex," Lyla stammered to introduce me.

The man in the suit stepped toward me and extended his hand. "Hey, Alex, glad you could come. I'm Lance." I shook his hand. "Come on in. This is my girlfriend, Irene. He pointed to the woman who had asked about me. *Good, he has a girlfriend, which means the kiss was just a friendly birthday greeting. The bartender was just a distraction. Let's see about the other two guys.*

"Beck, David, come over and introduce yourselves to Lyla's date."

"What? No, no, he's not my date." I noted that Lyla protested too much. She stepped between Lance and me, then she turned to me and mouthed, "Why are you here?"

I stepped closer to her and whispered, "My direct order was to keep you safe. I can't really keep you safe if I'm at home and you're at a club."

"I am safe. I'm with my friends," she whispered back.

Before I could reply, the two other guys approached us. Lyla smiled and introduced me. "Beck, this is Alex. David, this is Alex." I shook each of their hands. We exchanged pleasantries.

"Hey, I spoke to you on the phone," Beck said eagerly.

"You're the hacker?"

"Uh, are you sure I'm not in trouble?"

"I'm sure," I said, amused.

"Then, that I am. Great firewalls you guys have set up."

"Would you like something to drink before Beck shows you his geek card?" David asked me.

"I'll get it. Come on, Alex. Follow me to the bar," Lyla interrupted, and I followed her to the bar, which was unattended but well-stocked. "What can I get you?"

"I don't drink, and you're not safe here," I replied.

She still made me a gin and tonic and dropped a piece of lime into the glass. She smiled and handed the drink to me. "Here you go." She leaned in closer and whispered, "Alex, it's my birthday. All these people went to all this trouble to celebrate my birthday. I'm not in any danger. I've known these guys for a long time. There are no Pure Evils here. The worst they've done is, well," she paused and scanned the room. "Let's see, Lance has been ticketed for public nudity and disorderly conduct. Beck was caught hacking into some governmental agency, which he promised never to do again."

"I think he broke that promise."

"He promised not to hack into *that particular* agency."

"Oh, well then that makes it all right," I rebutted.

"So please, let me stay. Please."

"Evans, I'm not trying to ruin your birthday. I'm just trying to protect you."

"Right, protect me from embarrassing myself." She shot me a look.

I took a sip of the drink that was in my hand, grateful that it was readily available. "That came out wrong," I said, hoping she could see that I was being contrite.

"I'm starting to accept this whole"—she added air quotes as she continued her sentence—'We serve Good and fight Evil' thing." She took a sip of her own drink. "I also understand that my life will never be the same. So please let me have this one night to enjoy and pretend that I'm still normal."

"Fine, I'll just be the guy from work. Enjoy your night." I took another sip.

"I can't pretend to be normal while you're watching me."

I finished my drink and set it back on the bar. "I'll wait down-stairs." I got up to leave. I didn't want to admit it but it hurt that she didn't want me to be around. *Why does this hurt so much?* I asked myself.

"Wait." She grabbed my hand. Her hand was warm—I didn't want to let go. "Just stay. Battle of the bands is about to begin. You'll need another drink for this." I smiled and walked back.

"What would you like?"

"What you made me was pretty good."

"I thought you said you didn't drink."

"Is there singing involved?"

"Yeah, I better make you a double."

As soon as she set my drink down, Lance tugged on her arm. "Come on, Lyla, we're up first. We gotta set the standards high."

She wasn't half bad, even though she was playing a plastic gui-tar with buttons. The three guys and Lyla must be good friends. Her file didn't go into any great depths about her friendships and rela-tionships. But it looked like they played together quite often. Lance was singing. Beck was on the plastic drums, and David was playing a similar plastic guitar to the one Lyla was using. A score of 98 flashed on the screen.

"What? That was so 100 percent. Beck, your PlayStation is whacked!" Lance yelled in protest.

"There's nothing wrong with the PlayStation. Let a real girl group show you," Irene called out.

Group after group went up to play...or battle, if you want to call it that. Laughter and drinks kept going all night. People who worked at the club would come in and out to talk to Lance. Lance must run this place. That explained why he went in and out of the room.

A few girls tried to talk to me and asked me to go downstairs to the dance floor with them. I would look over at Lyla, but she was always speaking with someone, usually David or Beck. Though she did stop by to check on me a few times. I spent the rest of the night watching her.

I couldn't help myself; I found myself staring at Lyla like I was admiring a painting. Then for the second time since I met Lyla, I could feel emotions from her. I watched her across the room talking with a man and a woman. I could sense that she was feeling insecure, vulnerable, and hurt. She was jealous. She tried to avoid eye contact with either of them. Even though this person was standing next to a woman holding her hand, his body was leaning toward Lyla's. He was a little too comfortable, like it was natural for him to be close to her. I read his feelings; he was acknowledging Lyla's beauty and longing for her.

Lyla was standing straight and looking around the room. She's trying too hard to act casual, I thought. I could clearly sense that she wanted desperately for someone to save her.

I walked over and grabbed two glasses of champagne from the bar. I handed one to her and kissed her cheek. She looked at me briefly, hiding the shock on her face as quickly as possible.

"There you are." I reached out my hand. "Hi, I'm Alex. Thanks for keeping my girlfriend entertained."

"Matt, this is Alex. Alex, this is Matt, and this is Matt's girl-friend, Sheila." He was even more shocked than Lyla. They looked at each other. The look they had for each other, it was too familiar and too natural. I felt like I was hit in the gut. She shrugged her shoulders in response to his questioning gaze.

"Matt, how do you two know each other?" I asked, but I already knew the answer. Briefly, he tilted his head toward her. She shrugged again. All this nonverbal communication was starting to tick me off. I smiled, waiting for him to answer, as I put my arm around Lyla's waist and pulled her closer to me.

"Gosh, Matt and I have known each other a long time now," she replied, forcing a laugh.

Clearly annoyed, Sheila gave a deep sigh and pretended she was bored with the whole situation. "They used to go out." I could feel that she was irritated, but not from running into her boyfriend's ex but because I didn't acknowledge her physical beauty.

"Well, Matt, it's good to meet you, and I for one am glad that the two of you didn't work out. Well, enjoy your evening." I led Lyla to the other end of the room.

"You can let go of me now," she said quietly. I hesitated for a moment; I couldn't lie to myself, it felt good to hold her. I leaned in and whispered in her ear, "You can thank me later." Lyla rolled her eyes and walked off.

I found her standing alone on the fire escape. Her walls were still down, and I could clearly feel what she was feeling. She felt alone, betrayed, and hurt. However, a part of her also longed to be wanted by Matt. On cue, Matt joined her on the fire escape. I stood closer to the large window that opened to the fire escape. I didn't mean to eavesdrop, but I couldn't leave Lyla alone.

"Hi," Matt said, almost in a whisper. Lyla quickly turned around. She stepped to the side to make room for him. "I can tell you want to be alone, but I don't know when I'll get to see you again." Lyla didn't answer but straightened her back and stood taller. "I never got a chance to give you my condolences about your father." Again, Lyla didn't reply. "If you're not talking to me, it must mean that you still care enough about me to be mad at me," his voice trailed off at the end.

"Don't kid yourself." From where I was standing, I saw Lyla gently close her eyes, and a single tear fell down her cheek.

"I'm sorry, Lyla, I should have been there for you." Matt grabbed Lyla's hand and kissed the back of it. "Why didn't you tell me that your father was dying?" I wanted to punch him.

Lyla swallowed hard, took her hand back, and stepped away from Matt. "You were busy breaking up with me. I didn't want to interrupt."

"God, Lyla, I would have—"

"At least postponed breaking up with me until after the funeral," she interrupted. She looked away from him again. "I really needed you."

"I would have been there for you had I known." He turned her to face him. "It would have been good to be needed by you. All I ever wanted was to be needed by you. That's why I broke up with you. You never seem to need me or anyone."

Lyla gave him a small laugh and shook her head. "Then you never really knew me." She walked closer to the railing. "So you're telling me that had I been more clingy you wouldn't have broken up with me?" Lyla didn't wait for Matt to answer. "And Sheila?"

"She's not you." Matt shook his head. "I was never unfaithful to you. You gotta believe that." Matt grabbed Lyla's hands.

In a lackluster voice, Lyla replied, "Thank you for stopping by my house to dump me on your way to sleep with another woman."

"I know that saying sorry doesn't begin to make up for what I did. But I really do miss you. Is there any way you can give me another chance?" Lyla quickly backed away from Matt.

I stepped in. I think I was afraid to hear her answer. "Evans." She turned around and looked at me, quickly shutting down all her emotions. She is good at that. She smiled, but said nothing.

"Happy Birthday, Lyla. Please think about my question." Matt brushed past me.

"Are you okay?" She didn't answer me. "Oh, wait, is this a silent treatment? Are you mad at me too?"

"Were you listening to my conversation?" She didn't wait for me to reply. "Why should I be mad? I know you were just trying to help me. It's always awkward to run in to your old boyfriend and his new girlfriend. I figured I must have looked so desperate and pathetic that you actually took pity on me and helped me."

"You didn't look desperate or pathetic. Is that why you think I did that?" She didn't reply, and I had a feeling she wasn't going to answer my question. She just kept staring at the dark skies.

"Evans," I called out. "For the first time, I could feel emotions, real emotions from you, besides when you're alone in your room." She turned her head and looked at me with embarrassment. We both knew what I was referring to.

With an even tone, she finally spoke. "Alex, you're an Empath. You're supposed to read my emotions."

"That's just it. You have built so many walls around you, I can't. God, Lyla, you are the first person I can't read very well."

"I know, you told me."

"I did?" I was puzzled. I didn't remember telling her.

"I thought you did. Maybe it was just a dream."

"You dream about me?" Lyla's expression changed. I had clearly caught her off guard.

In a loud voice mixed with fake laughter, she said, "No, of course not, that would be silly." She let out a breath that she'd been holding for a while and turned around to go back into the room. She paused to face me and said, "Thank you." She walked away before I could even reply. Just like that, our conversation was over. *She is so damn frustrating.*

Finally, the DJ called for last call. Lance pulled out some shot glasses and called everyone to the bar. He liberally poured from a very expensive bottle of tequila. "Everyone take a glass. I want to make a toast to my good friend, Lyla." I noticed that Irene came closer to his side and put an arm around his waist. He gave her a kiss to make her feel less jealous. *Girls and their pettiness.*

"Irene, make him stop." Lyla declared with sleepy eyes. Irene shrugged her shoulders and raised her arms signaling that she was helpless.

"Lyla, you are my best friend…even though you don't consider me your best friend and I have to stand in line behind these two losers over here." He pointed at David and Beck. Both of them replied a protest. "Just for that sorry situation, we should drink to me." The crowd laughed, and Lance downed his drink in one gulp, then everyone followed suit. He asked everyone to put their glasses down on the bar, and he refilled them.

Lance cleared his throat, "Where was I? Oh yeah, you're my best friend and I know that you always have my back. That's a lot for a girl, you know. I've told you things that I would never tell these two losers."

"Dude, who are you calling a loser?" Beck replied and snorted. Everyone laughed.

Lance pointed to himself and then to Beck and David, "We're lucky to have a friend like you. Happy 23rd birthday and many more to come! I hope we can always celebrate it with you."

The three guys gave her a hug. *I guess they are all just friends.* I was relieved. Outside the club, the air felt good on my face. Beck, David, and I were carrying all the gifts that Lyla had received. Lance stayed in the club to help close down. "Am I taking you home?" David asked.

Lyla looked at me briefly. "No, uh, Alex and I drove here together straight from work. I should probably get my car."

"It's almost three, why don't I just take you later to pick up your car?" Lyla blinked her eyes. She was too tired and had had too much drink to think of another excuse.

"She left her car at my house. I had to go home and change first. Don't worry. I'll get her a cup of coffee first before I send her home," I said, stepping in.

"Yeah, that's it," she added.

"Lyla," David pronounced her name slowly. *David's playing the big brother act.*

"Da–a–vid," she replied. "It will be okay, and I will call you as soon as I get home."

"Fine, Alex, where did you park?"

As soon as he asked, the valet pulled up with my car. The valet clicked the button to open the trunk and handed me the keys with a big smile. "Man, she's a beauty. Hands down, the best car in the lot tonight," he announced with excitement.

I placed the gifts in the trunk and gave him a tip. Beck and David placed the gifts they were carrying in the trunk as well.

Beck inspected my car as he walked around it. "Dude, are you kidding me? You drive a 2015 Audi R8. You know it's 2012 and your car is a 2015. How is that possible?

"I'm testing it out," I replied nonchalantly.

Beck walked closer to me. "Can you drive me home? Or if you want, I'll go home with you if you let me drive."

We all chuckled.

Lyla was asleep when we pulled up to the house. I didn't want to wake her up. I just sat there watching her sleep. About half an hour later, she woke up, "We're home? I mean we're here at your house. Why didn't you just wake me up?"

"We just got here," I lied. I opened the door and swung around the car to open her door for her. She was putting her shoes back on. She stepped out of the car and winced.

"I never want to walk in these shoes ever again. After wearing them all night, it's like stepping on needles." She took off her shoes again and walked to the house barefoot.

"Careful, it's a bit slippery in some places."

"Alex, your garage is spotless." As soon as she said that, she slipped on a small pool of oil that had accumulated from a leak from an old Indian motorcycle that I have been restoring.

I quickly held her at the waist to stop her from falling.

"Thanks, I guess. You saved me from embarrassing myself." She almost broke a leg and still managed to take a jab at me.

"About that, I didn't mean it that way. I saw that bartender touching you and flirting with you and you were…" I didn't want to finish my sentence.

"What? What was I doing?" She demanded.

"You were flirting back?" I quickly replied.

"I know," she said, looking down. "I was trying to make Matt jealous. I'm not proud of myself, but I'm a girl. Can you blame me?"

"You walked away together alone. You could have been in danger."

"In danger?" Lyla gave a small laugh.

"Well, yeah, he looked sinister."

"Tyler is not sinister. He just wants to sleep with every girl he meets."

"So you would have slept with him, just to make your ex-boyfriend jealous."

I saw anger flash in her eyes. "I never said that, and anyway it is none of your business. You can let go of me." I looked down at my hands, which were still around her waist.

"Sorry." I was embarrassed. I didn't even realize that I hadn't let go of her, or maybe I didn't want to let go of her. I ran my fingers through my hair and gave her a smile that showed my dimples. I hadn't used this trick since I was boy trying to get out of a punishment from my grandmother.

"Whatever; I'm going to bed." She walked into the house. I followed quietly, not daring to say anymore. I watched her go up the stairs holding on to the railing I had installed while we were in San Francisco.

Maybe I'm losing my touch. I can't believe my smile didn't work.

"And thank you for installing the railings!" She yelled out when she reached the top of the stairs. I heard her slam her door. *At least the damn railings scored some points.*

As soon as I lay on the bed, I knew I wouldn't be able to sleep. I felt bad that I forgot it was her birthday. That must have been Lupe's message to me that I never bothered to listen to. I got out of bed and checked my messages. Sure enough, one of them was from Lupe letting me know it was Lyla's birthday today. I slammed the phone down. Lyla must think I don't care. *But I don't, right?* I asked myself. After all, she's just another assignment. I just need to keep her safe, that's all. So why did I find myself softly knocking on her door? "Evans, are you sleeping?"

"No, come in." I walked in, but stopped by the doorway. "Is there something wrong?" She was already in bed. I could tell that I woke her up. She switched on the lamp next to her bed.

"I'm sorry. You were already sleeping. I just felt bad that I didn't get you anything for your birthday. So…" I paused and rested my hands on my thighs. "I, uh…" I ran my fingers through my hair. *God, I am nervous.* "Just wait; it won't take long." I ran back to my room and picked up my guitar. I tried to walk back to her room as calmly as possible. I didn't remember ever being so nervous. *Dammit, what am I doing?*

I sat at the edge of her bed. She was already in a sitting position. Her eyes were following me patiently. I started strumming the chords, making sure my guitar was tuned. *Why didn't I do this before I came storming into her room? God, why am I doing this at all?* Satisfied that I was ready, I started humming the first few chords and then the first few words. My voiced cracked. *Oh shit, maybe I should just give up now.* I looked up and she gave me a warm smile. *Please let that smile be just for me.* I started over and sang "Somewhere Over the Rainbow" not daring to look at her until the end of the song.

She clapped. "I love that song! How did you know?" She jumped out of the covers and gave me a hug. I barely had time to put the guitar down. Her abilities were growing stronger, but I don't think she realized that she leaped over to me faster than an average human being would've been able to. She felt warm, and the hairs on the back of my neck responded to her touch. Her embrace felt so good. I didn't want to let go.

"I just guessed, since you wake up to it every morning." I distanced myself a little bit from her, signaling the end of our embrace. She took the hint and let go of me. I saw a flash of disappointment on her face. She felt regret. *Does she regret hugging me?* Not as much as I regretted letting her go, but if I didn't, I wasn't sure I could restrain myself any longer from doing what I really wanted to do. "Well, good night and happy birthday." I walked out of her room. In the hallway, I stopped to hit my head on the wall. *Someone shoot me now. That was embarrassing...and what were all those papers taped to the wall in her room?*

chapter

TWENTY FIVE

Lyla

It was almost noon when I woke up, and I immediately wondered if I had dreamed that Alex came into my room and sang me a song. *It must have been a dream.*

I lay in bed for a while, deep under the covers, thinking about my actions. Yesterday I had sneaked out of the house, and I felt bad. With all of the crazy things that had happened to me, I had forgotten about my twenty-third birthday until Beck spilled the beans about my surprise party. I knew I had to go.

It would have severely disappointed Lance if I didn't show up. Lance doesn't do too well with disappointments or feeling rejected. He had a rough time growing up. His father was an alcoholic and a gambler who eventually went to jail. His mother left shortly afterward, leaving him with an aunt and uncle who weren't interested in raising him. He had learned not to place himself in situations where anyone had the opportunity to hurt him. So throwing a birthday party for me was a big deal for Lance. He was probably trying to make up for the fact that it was my first birthday without my father.

I heard my stomach grumble. I was hungry. I stretched and got out of bed. The sun was too bright, so I left my eyes closed as I headed to the bathroom to take a shower. I started taking my shirt off when I heard someone clear his throat.

It was Alex. "Hi. I should have probably said something sooner." I was thankful that my back was turned to him. I quickly struggled to put my shirt back on, but my arm got stuck in the opening that was meant for my head. I tried to find the door to the bathroom and ended up banging my head on the door.

"Ouch!" That sent a rush of pain, and I realized that I had drunk too much last night. My head was throbbing.

Alex laughed. "Slow down; I promise I'm facing the wall and didn't see anything."

I finally managed to put my shirt back on. I turned to him— he had kept his word and was facing the wall. "Why are you in my room? I mean I know it's your house, but…"

"I tried to wait until you woke up, but it's already noon and there were no signs that you were going to wake up any time soon. I wanted to see what you had posted all over the wall."

"I'm sorry. I should have asked first. I hope that's okay. I've been trying to analyze what connections I have with all of this," I explained, throwing my arms as wide as possible. "The answer is here somewhere. I know it. My gut feeling is telling me." On cue, my stomach growled again.

Alex laughed, "I think I know what your stomach is telling you. There's food in the kitchen, and Father wants to talk to us. We'll leave in an hour."

"How come you call him Father, not Dad or Daddy?"

Alex gave me a blank look.

"It's just so formal, so Charles Ingalls. You know what I mean?"

"No, I don't know what you mean. Half the time, I'm not really sure what you're talking about. One hour."

"Okay," I said, feeling deflated. It was definitely a dream.

I quickly showered and changed. I devoured the food Flora had left for me. I guess I was hung over and my body needed the food. I wanted to take a nap, and Alex's couch looked so inviting. I was just about to walk over to his living room when he walked in.

"Ready?"

"Ready," I said, yawning.

We were both quiet during the drive to the office. In the elevator, I had expected to go down again, but the elevator went up to the top floor.

The older woman I had met my first day was sitting behind a reception desk. She looked up when we approached her desk. "Good morning, Mr. St James. Ms. Evans. I see you met Alex."

"Yes, I did." I smiled, and she returned my smile.

"Alex, your father is waiting for you." She gestured to a set of double doors.

I walked closer to Alex and whispered, "I take it she doesn't work in our department?"

Alex smiled at me and it made my stomach felt weird. *Oh, that smile and those dimples.* He opened the door for me. Alex's father sat behind a massive desk. Windows covered every inch of his huge office. There was a man sitting in one of the chairs in front of his desk. Two men in black suits stood by the double doors.

Alex's father stood up, "Ah, there they are." Alex led me to the empty chair in front of his father's desk. "Ms. Evans, please have a seat."

I stood in front of Alex's father and greeted him, "Good morning, Mr. St. James."

"Please, I feel like were old friends. Call me Martin." I sat down. "I was just having a chat with an acquaintance of yours."

I turned to the man sitting next to me and jumped out of my seat. "Beck!" I instantly became worried and scanned his arms and face, checking for any wounds or bruises. "Are you okay?" I was relieved to find none. I gave him a hug. Beck was wearing a uniform from a cable company.

"Yeah, Lyla, I'm okay." Beck flinched. He was embarrassed that I was fussing over him.

"Sorry, I pulled out the mom card," I leaned over and whispered to him.

"It's okay." Nervous, we both leaned back in our chairs.

"It seems that our young friend has visited our building before unannounced and in false pretense as a representative from a cable company." Martin sat back in his chair as well. Alex remained quiet standing next to me.

"That was my fault. I asked him to. I can explain." I leaned over to Beck again and whispered, "Where did you get the uniform?"

Beck smiled. "Irene's brother got a job with Charter cable. I'm borrowing it. I promised to have it dry cleaned before giving it back."

"Oh, okay. I'll do that for you. Sorry about this," I whispered back.

Alex cleared his throat. "Evans, do you want to explain why you had a need to ask your friend to hack into our systems?"

I was quiet for a moment. "I, uh, well, you see."

"Cause one of you is trying to hurt Lyla," Beck announced in a clear voice.

"It is unfortunate that someone is trying to hurt you, Ms. Evans, but rest assured that we are doing everything we can to protect you as well as find the person responsible for these despicable acts against you," Martin explained.

"Unless it's you who wants to hurt Lyla...then you wouldn't really be trying so hard." Beck gripped my hand. There was only one other time he had held my hand: during high school. We were at a pool hall and Lance started a fight with an Asian gang. Beck held my hand as a signal for me to get ready to run.

"You need to be very careful about what you say next," Alex said in a terse voice.

"It's okay, Alex. Mr. Ford, would you care to explain why you are accusing me?"

Beck didn't let go of my hand. "Well, it is either you, a woman named Marsha Lee Bardot, or Liam Rogets."

"What are you trying to say?" Alex was starting to become impatient.

"Each of you has had business meetings or made travel plans near the vicinity of the murders that Lyla has been researching. Each of you has accessed and viewed the file on Lyla."

"There's a file on me?"

"Oh yeah, it goes all the way back to your childhood. Even what diapers you used to use."

"Okay, I got it."

"And that guy," Beck tilted his head toward Alex, "has opened it at least thirty-three times since I last checked."

Alex's face was stoic. "Is that how you know I like vanilla ice cream?" I asked, turning away from Alex.

Alex didn't answer. Martin looked up toward the two men who were still standing by the door. "Gentlemen, I'm sure you have other things you need to attend to. Thank you for bringing Mr. Ford to my office." The men left.

I looked over at Beck. "They were the ones who caught me."

"Ms. Evans, it appears that I owe you an explanation."

"Lyla, just Lyla."

"All right. Lyla." Martin smiled at me. "It has been my pleasure to look after you."

"What?"

"I knew your mother, Delilah."

"My mother?" Alex placed his hand on my shoulder. I shrugged it off.

"We were old friends. Shortly after you were born, she came to me and asked me to, well, she made me promise to look after you. I have fulfilled my promise."

"Spying on me?"

"No, just making sure you were safe." Martin walked around the desk. "Would you like me to show you?"

I nodded. He placed his hand on mine. Images of my second grade teacher, our mailman, the sous chef at my father's restaurant, and even the babysitter my father often used came rushing into my mind.

"I see. Where is my mother now?"

"I honestly don't know, dear. I haven't seen Delilah or spoken to her since the night she asked me to look after you. She was disturbed and anxious, but she refused to tell me anything else."

I wanted so badly to ask him to show me an image of my mother, but I became fearful. It had been so long since I talked about my mother. My mind went blank. I tried to recite my table of two's but all the energy in me seemed to have left my body. My head still hurt from all the alcohol I had consumed last night. I couldn't stop thinking about the question I have lived with all my life: *Why did my mother leave me?*

No one said anything for a while. I stared at my hands. Alex finally broke the silence. "I'm going to take her home."

"I'm sorry, Alex, just a few more minutes. There is something that I must ask of Lyla's friend."

I looked at Martin and then at Beck. "It appears that you have helped us narrow down the list of suspects. Unfortunately, the list of suspects isn't that narrow. We have silent partners who have also traveled the same places that myself, Dr. Rogets and Ms. Bardot." Martin turned to me. "I would not presume to ask you to believe that I would never hurt you. I do think that your friend can help prove my innocence."

"What do you want me to do?" Beck asked.

"To use your skills, Mr. Ford. I need you to hack into someone's laptop."

"You have a whole IT department, why do you need me?"

"It seems that I have found myself in a predicament where I cannot trust anyone in the company. I am very saddened about it."

"You mean the guy who hacked into Lyla's computer." Martin nodded his head.

"If I do this, then Lyla is free to leave this guy's house?" Beck pointed at Alex.

"I'm sorry, that is out of the question. We cannot do that until we can ensure that Ms. Evans is safe. I promised her mother. But I can offer you something else." Martin pushed a manila file, an inch thick, toward Beck. I peered over when Beck opened the file, and from my limited view, I assumed it was his court records.

Beck quickly placed the file back on the desk. He became quiet and reserved, just like the old Beck I remembered who transferred into my high school our freshman year. I opened the file and discovered that I was right, it was his court records. I flipped to the bottom of the file. It included his arrest records for hacking into government agencies and his time in foster care and group homes.

"How did you get this?" I asked.

Martin didn't answer my question and continued to speak with Beck. "In return for your special service, I will make sure that this is all erased." He tapped his finger on the file.

"What about Lyla? I want her to be able to go where she pleases."

"You do this, and we'll be closer to finding out who wants to hurt her." Beck and Martin stared at each other.

I pulled on Beck's t-shirt sleeve. "It's not that bad, staying at Alex's house. Free meals, wi-fi, and a large Jacuzzi bath tub. It's like staying at a five-star hotel for free."

"Sure?"

"Yeah." I turned to Martin. "How much danger is he putting himself in?"

"Little to none; I just need him to do what he does best."

"He won't be in any danger?"

"There are always certain risks," Martin replied without any emotions.

Beck shrugged. "Fine, but you need to tell me how you plan on making all of this go away." It was Beck's turn to tap on the file.

"I have certain connections."

"I see." Beck stared out the window. It reminded me of how we first met. In English class, we were both staring out the same window. We caught each other staring out into the world, not paying attention to the teacher. I smiled and he smiled back, and we've been friends ever since. "I'll do it. Who owns this laptop and where is it?"

"The man who owns the laptop is Nolan Gray, and he is currently in Hawaii."

"Father," Alex interrupted.

"What? Who is Nolan Gray? Is he dangerous?" I asked anxiously.

"He can be. Father, I'm going with him."

"Me too. I'm going," I said raising my hand.

"No, it's too dangerous. I don't want you anywhere near that guy." Alex reached for my hand and put it down.

Mimicking his father, I said, "Alex, there are always certain risks."

Martin laughed. "I had heard about your sense of humor. I was hoping that all of you would go."

"Father, no, it's too dangerous."

"Hawaii! Sweet," Beck declared. "Can we fly first class? Okay, at least business class, since it is business, right?"

"That's the spirit. Just think of it as a paid vacation," Martin replied.

chapter

TWENTY SIX

Lyla

An hour later, we were boarding a private jet headed toward Hawaii. I didn't see Ben. Two different pilots greeted us this time, and there was a flight attendant with us on board. Beck was like a kid in a candy store—or, really, Beck looked like what he usually looked like at an Apple store. He checked everything out in the plane and ordered everything the flight attendant offered. I asked for two aspirins and a bottle of water.

I stared out of the window. After an hour in the air, Alex sat down across from me. I looked up to face him. "I'm sorry about the file." He looked down at his hands. "I know we invaded your privacy."

"I had a feeling."

"How?"

"Besides the vanilla ice cream. The song."

"Last night?"

"Yeah, I stopped listening to that song when my father died. He used to sing it in the mornings while he made me breakfast."

"I'm really sorry. And about viewing your files...a few times."

"Thirty-three times." I looked up to check his face. I saw a slight blush in his cheeks.

"Yeah, about that, it was just, you know research, since I'm in charge of your safety."

"Of course, research. Did you know that your father knew my mother?"

"No, he's never mentioned you or your mother before." Alex looked out the window. "I wish he did. We could have met sooner." He didn't wait for me to reply and kept talking. "Here's a file on Nolan. You might want to read it. It could be useful." I took the file and our fingers touched slightly, resulting in a warm, funny feeling in my stomach. We both looked up at each other. Alex quickly pulled his hand away, "Right, I'm gonna see if there's any coffee. Do you want a cup?" He stood up and walked away.

"Yeah, a cup of coffee sounds good." I wasn't sure if he heard me. I turned to face the window. Alex didn't sit near me for the remainder of our flight. The flight attendant brought me my coffee.

A black Mercedes-Benz was waiting for us when we landed. "I like it," Beck said, with a big thumbs up.

"I'll sit in the back, Beck." I knew Beck would want shotgun. Beck found a pair of aviator sunglasses in the glove compartment. "This is the life," he commented as he put the glasses on.

When we finally pulled up to the resort we were staying at, Beck announced, "No, *this* is the life." The resort was enormous.

In the lobby, I noticed the back of a man's profile that looked familiar. He had his arms around two women wearing swimsuits. He turned to us and said, "Welcome." It was Riley. He whispered in both the girls' ears, and they walked away. "See you in a bit, girls," he called. "You must be Beck, nice to meet you." He shook hands with Beck.

A woman dressed in the resort's uniform walked toward us. She welcomed us and gave each of a us lei and our room key cards.

"Thank you," Riley spoke for us. "Come on, I have cocktails ready." He led us over to the bar near the swimming pool.

I groaned at the thought of more alcohol. Riley passed me a white blended drink with a pink umbrella. "No more," I waved it away. "Wait—oh, it looks so good," I grabbed the drink from Riley's hand.

"You had enough last night." Alex took the drink from me.

Alex placed the drink back down on the bar. "I just want to taste it," I protested and grabbed the straw with my lips to sip my drink as fast as I could. I placed my hand on my head, "Oh, brain freeze."

"Don't you hate it when that happens?" Beck had a coconut drink in each of his hands. He alternated sipping from each drink.

"Are we sipping cocktails for a reason?" Alex asked Riley.

"Of course, what else goes with cocktails by the pool but a little recon? Our guy is right there, corner of the pool, wearing a tacky swimsuit and chatting up a brunette in a green swimsuit."

We all turned our heads. "Bloody hell, don't all look at the same time." Riley's accent came out. We quickly turned our heads the other way.

"Let's head to our room before he notices us." Alex started walking back to the lobby. Our rooms were next to each other. Since we didn't bring anything, we didn't have much to put away. Five minutes after checking out our rooms, we found ourselves in Riley's room, which was a suite that included a large sitting room, dining room, and a bar. Room service was already waiting for us in the room.

"What's the plan?" I asked between bites of my sandwich.

Alex was staring out the window at the view of the pool and the ocean. He walked back to the couch and picked up the last plate of food. Although I'd been staying at his house for a while, I realized that this was the first time I had seen Alex eat. We had never actually shared a meal together. "Simple. We distract him. Get his laptop from his room, and Beck can do his thing."

"How do we distract him?" I asked.

"He seems to be distracted by brunettes," Riley chimed in.

"I don't usually like sandwiches, but this is delicious." I said, wiping sauce from the corner of my mouth. I looked up and all three pairs of eyes were looking at me.

I turned to Beck and asked, "What, do I have sauce on my face?"

"No, but I think they want you to distract him."

"Sure, how?"

"Just by being your lovely self," Riley answered.

"What does that mean?" I put my plate down.

"Just chat with him by the pool," Riley explained.

"Sorry, I didn't bring my bathing suit. What's plan B?"

"We can't bloody blow up the hotel now, can we?" Riley's English accent wasn't so cute anymore.

"Of course not, silly. That's plan C," I said we a fake smile. There was a knock on the door. Riley stood up to open it. Lupe and Amanda walked in, each with a rolling suitcase.

"Someone called for room service?" Lupe announced.

"How does she do that?" Riley asked.

I introduced Beck to Lupe and Amanda. Lupe's suitcase was full of technology. Beck's face looked like he'd just won the lottery. Technology was the only thing that could make Beck put his food down. He began setting up the equipment right away.

Amanda placed her suitcase on the couch. "Would you prefer the classic black bikini or are you in a daring mood?" Amanda lifted up a very small two-piece black bikini and an even smaller white bikini.

I inquired about a bathing suit that would cover a little more of me. "Is there a one-piece?"

"Sorry, the eight-year-old girls took the last one," Amanda replied with sarcasm in her voice.

"How the hell is she supposed to hide any weapons wearing a string bikini?" We all turned to Alex, surprised by his question and his outburst.

I could feel Amanda staring at me and waiting for my response. Shrugging my shoulders, I said, "I just ate the best pulled pork sandwich for lunch."

"Black it is," Amanda replied, shoving the bathing suit toward me.

Beck was staring at one of the computer screens, "You better get out there fast. It looks like the target is done doing laps in the pool."

"Fine," I said, taking the swimsuit from Amanda. "Let's see what this guy looks like." I said walking over to one of the monitors. "Did you hack into the hotel's surveillance system?"

"You know it. Up top." I gave Beck a high five and glanced at the computer screen just in time for me to see our target get out of the pool. My jaw dropped as I stared and checked him out. To sum it up, he was hot. The water from the pool made his blond hair glisten under the sun. His abs were ridiculous. I motioned for Lupe to come over.

"Hot damn! Now, that's a target." I was so focused on the freedom that I had to check out this guy on the video that I didn't notice at first that Amanda had joined us. "He's sexier than you, Amanda."

"There's no need for exaggeration," Amanda chimed in, and all three of us giggled.

Beck said, "It's a good thing I'm not wearing my trunks. You ladies wouldn't be able to handle all of this." He rubbed his belly. We laughed harder.

"Ladies, do you want to focus? We are here for a mission." Alex put our laughter to a halt.

"I'll go change." I got up and walked past Amanda's suitcase. I saw a floral sarong and grabbed it. "I'm taking this." I announced to Amanda.

"That's not the image I was going for," she called out after me.

I changed into the bathing suit that I would definitely never, ever buy for myself. I looked at my reflection in the mirror. I sucked in my gut, put the sarong on, and rushed out.

"All right, let's go," I announced. I didn't like being the only one in the room wearing a bathing suit while everyone else was fully clothed.

Riley whistled like a truck driver. "Oh, stop it. Okay, keep going," I joked with Riley, and everyone in the room laughed except for Alex, of course. "Let's go before I lose my nerve."

In the elevator, I got some last-minute directions from Riley. "Don't worry, I'll figure out a way to get a mic near you so that we can hear everything you're talking about. You'll be great." He patted my head and got out on the floor that he had designated the elevator to stop on.

I felt a momentary awkwardness when the elevator doors shut and it was just Alex and me. One floor later, Alex spoke up, "Don't be afraid. Remember, Beck and Lupe have eyes on you."

"Right," I said, nodding.

"And you may not see me, but I'll always be there for you." He turned to me and readjusted my sarong to cover more of my thigh. He grabbed my shoulders and said, "Don't ever doubt that." Before I could react, the elevator doors opened onto the lobby. He motioned for me to go out first. I headed to the double doors leading to the pool, and Alex went the other direction.

No turning back now, Lyla, I said to myself. Remembering that our target had a certain taste for expensive cars, I decided to buy some car magazines from the store lobby before proceeding out to the pool. If nothing else, I could at least use them to hide my face.

There was one empty lounge chair next to our target. He was lying on his back. I quickly sat down, trying very hard not to look at him. I opened the magazine and pretended to read as I focused on slowing down my breathing. A few minutes later—I'm sure it was only a few minutes, but it felt like a lifetime—a hotel employee with serving trays walked up to the space between me and our target.

"Mojito," the employee announced, lowering his tray. It took a fraction of a second to realize that it was Riley. Seizing the opportunity to initiate contact, I reached for the drink at the same time that our target reached for the glass. Our fingers briefly touched.

"Oh, excuse me," I said, quickly letting go of the drink and breaking contact with our target. "I'm so sorry. I thought it was my drink."

"It might be," our target replied, sitting up. "Please, take it," he said, taking the drink from the tray.

"Miss, did you order a mojito as well?" Riley asked me.

"Yes, yes, I did."

"I'll get another right away," Riley replied, nodding, and walked away.

"Well, there you go, problem solved. In the meantime, please take the drink. It would be a shame to have someone as lovely as you wait for a drink."

"All right, I'll take the drink, but only because that was probably one of the cheesiest lines I have ever heard." I was about to take a sip of the drink when I noticed a tiny black object on the top of my straw. *This might be the mic.* I imagined Beck rolling his eyes at our target's cheesy line.

He chuckled at my response. "I'm Nolan, and you are?"

Shit, name. No one told me if I should use my real name or make up a fake name.

"Lola, my name is Lola. It's nice to meet you, Nolan." I shook his hand.

"Lola, are you here on vacation?"

"No, for work. And you?"

"I had to meet a man about a job."

"Great place for a job interview."

"You could say that."

I deliberately did not reply. I picked up my magazine and pretended to read. A moment later, Nolan asked, "Do you like cars?"

I gave what I thought was my 'oh, you got me' laugh. "It's kind of embarrassing actually." I placed the magazine down on my lap and angled myself to face him. "I was just reading it so I can pretend to know something about cars." I saw the confusion on our target's face. "It's really silly and stupid."

"Now I'm curious. Please go on."

"Are you sure you want to hear it?" I paused, and his body, which was now also aligned directly to mine, made me hopeful that I had his full attention.

Don't screw this up, Lyla. "I'm here for work and traveling with coworkers. I never seem to have anything to say to one particular coworker, and it's a long flight home. He's into cars, so I figured if we can at least talk about cars then maybe...just maybe..." I paused for a second. "I told you it was silly."

He smiled. "So you have a crush on your colleague."

"No," I said too loudly. "Of course not," I turned my body away from him and picked up the magazine again. After a moment, I said, "Oh my God, is it that obvious?" I buried my head in the magazine.

He laughed again. I had to admit that his laugh was sexy. "I want to meet this colleague."

I looked up and saw Alex and Amanda walking over to us. My eyes widened. This wasn't part of the plan. "Oh, that could be arranged," I said with a degree of worry in my voice. "Please, please promise me that you won't say anything. He's coming this way. Please." I clasped my fingers together and made a pleading motion.

"What will you do for me?"

"Huh?"

"If I do this for you, you'll have to do something for me in exchange."

"What?" I asked, pretending I was annoyed with his request. I raised the magazine to my face once again.

"Lola," I pretended to be surprised to see Alex and Amanda.

"Oh, hi there, Fred," quickly thinking of the dorkiest name I could come up with.

"I thought that was you. Sheila and I were going to head to town for dinner. Did you want to come?" On cue, Amanda linked her arm with his. It didn't escape me that she was wearing the white bikini that I didn't dare to wear. *Sheila, of all the names to pick from, he chose, Sheila. That's just low.*

"These must be your colleagues that you were telling me about," our target chimed in before I could answer.

"Ah, yes, Nolan, these are my coworkers, Fred and Sheila."

"Nice to meet you both. Lola actually has plans tonight," he gave me a look. "She just agreed to have dinner with me. I hope you don't mind."

Alex smiled, "No, not at all. It'll give you some more time to get to know each other a little more." I read between the lines. They needed more time to hack into the laptop.

Amanda turned to Alex and said, "We should get going. We don't want to be late for our dinner reservation." I noticed that their arms were still linked together even as they walked away. I knew that we were just pretending, but I felt a tiny pang of jealousy, which I quickly checked.

I leaned in and asked Nolan, "When did I agree to have dinner with you?"

He gave me a naughty grin. I wonder if that's the same smile that he uses to lure girls and sell them to the highest bidder. I suddenly felt sick at the thought of the countless of women who had become his victims and gotten stuck in the world of human trafficking.

"Lola?"

"What?" I said, realizing that I had gone out of character. I felt myself losing the façade that I had built up. Thankfully, at that moment, Riley showed up, still dressed as a waiter. "I'm sorry it took so long," he said, placing the glass in my hand and giving me a quick eye contact. I knew that I wasn't alone.

"We should probably get ready for dinner as well. We don't want to be late for our reservation," Nolan said, mimicking Amanda.

"Where are we going?" I asked, hoping to let the rest know about our destination.

"It's a surprise." I felt doomed again, realizing that I would be alone with this man during dinner.

I faked a smile. We gathered our things and parted in the lobby. Nolan explained that he had to check on a few things and asked me to be ready in an hour and meet him outside the front entrance. I went directly to my room and suppressed my need to run to Riley's room, where I knew everyone was waiting. Where I knew I would be safe. I took a shower, pausing now and then to take deep breaths. I dressed in a simple, short black cotton dress and sandals that Amanda had left for me. The length of the dress and flat sandals gave me mobility in case I needed to run for my life. I wanted to be as practical as possible; I figured I did my job by getting him out of his hotel room. I didn't need to wear heels and uncomfortable clothing to continue impressing him.

I wanted to back out. This would be a really good time to have Lupe around to calm my nerves. But part of the plan was no contact just in case Nolan checked on me. I took a deep breath, said a quick prayer, and headed down to the lobby. Nolan was already waiting for me in a convertible Ferrari. He was dressed in fitted, dark button-down shirt. His hair was styled, and it made him look even more handsome.

I smiled as I walked over to his car. Nolan didn't bother getting out to open the door for me. One of the valet guys did it. If this were a real date, I would have counted that as strike one. *But this isn't a date, Lyla. Focus.*

"Hi, you look nice," he said, taking off fast from the driveway of the hotel.

"You, too," I said, buckling up. Strike two, he didn't even wait for me to put my seatbelt on before he started driving. *Not a date, not a date. Dammit, focus.* "I see you like cars. I'm an avid reader of sports cars myself. But I won't bore you about just how much I know." He looked at me and started laughing.

"You're funny, Lola."

"It helps to mask my awkwardness of going on a date with a perfect stranger."

"Then let's get to know each other a little more," he said as he sped up.

Half an hour later, we pulled off the road and turned onto a gravel road that led to the only house or structure I could see for miles. "We're here." I looked around in the darkness. I could hear the ocean nearby.

"Where is here?"

"You'll see. Come on." He took my hand and led me up the house. I thought about shaking his hand away, but I had a feeling that he wasn't use to being rejected. I was glad that at least the house was well lit and there seemed to be at least one or two other people inside.

As we walked up the steps to the door, a woman in a black wraparound dress and sensible shoes opened the door to greet us. "Welcome, Mr. Gray. Your table is ready for you and your guest."

He led me inside one of the most charming restaurants I had ever seen. The house had been converted to a restaurant. There were a few tables set up with lit candles in what used to be the living room. There was a huge bay window on the far wall of the house. I could hear the waves lapping over each other. I quickly realized that the house was a few feet away from the beach.

"Where are the rest of the customers?" I whispered to Nolan as we followed the woman who greeted us.

"I don't like eating in crowded places," he whispered back. The woman led us out the back porch, through a small garden, and onto the beach. There was a table and two chairs set up on the sand, and torches were placed in the sand to make a walkway to the table.

"Oh my," I said, taking my seat. "Nolan, this is really nice."

"I'm glad you like it."

"Your first course will arrive momentarily," the woman said, handing Nolan a bottle of wine.

Nolan accepted the bottle and looked at the label, saying, "This is fine." She took the bottle back and set it on a smaller table that was set up off to the side. I saw several other bottles of wine on the table. I figured they were ready in case Nolan didn't approve of their first choice.

She returned with the bottle uncorked and poured our wine glasses. Two men came just as she finished pouring my wine. They placed the plates at the same time, stood to the side, and took the metal domes from our plates in a synchronous motion.

"Please enjoy," the woman said to us.

"Thank you for taking me here," I said, genuinely touched by his effort.

The food was delicious, and I was surprised to discover that I didn't have to try all that hard to have a conversation with Nolan. He was easy to talk to and equally carried the conversation. He was open, and he freely shared about his childhood as well as embarrassing stories from his awkward teenage years. I told him that I had a hard time picturing him as an awkward teenager who was shy around girls. He confessed that he didn't believe me when I said I had to make an effort to strike up a conversation my coworker.

Two bottles of wine later, we headed back to the hotel. I only hoped that was enough time for Beck to hack into his laptop. I couldn't drink one more glass and be held accountable for my actions. We pulled up to the driveway of the hotel, and he tossed his keys to the valet. I still wasn't sure how I was going to end this night. In the elevator, he pressed the button for the elevator to stop at his floor, since it was nowhere near my room. He placed his arm around my shoulder and kissed my ear, slowly working his way down my neck. *Oh, shit, I didn't think about this part. I didn't ask if there was an extraction plan.* I could feel the butterflies in my stomach.

Thank goodness, the elevator doors opened before he could kiss me any lower on my chest. We walked down the hallway, and the only other person in the hallway was a hotel employee carrying some pillows and bed sheets. As we got a little closer, I realized it was Lupe. I quickly looked back and she put five fingers up. *What does that mean? They aren't done and need five more minutes? Oh, shit. This is getting worse.*

We must've been close to his room, because he took a key card from his pocket. I panicked and stopped. This forced him to turn around and look at me. I didn't realize that my mouth had gone so dry, and I had to lick my lips before I could even speak. "I really had a wonderful time tonight. Everything was perfect. Thank you." He regarded me. It felt like it was the first time that he really was looking at me.

"I should be the one thanking you. You're special, Lola. I had forgotten that girls like you exist."

"Girls like me?"

"Yes, girls like you." Out of the corner of my eye, I saw a door slightly opening and Riley's head pop out for a second. Desperate, I stood on my tiptoes and kissed his lips gently. That wasn't so bad, I thought. He took the kiss for more than what I intended it to be. He cupped my face with both his hands and kissed me hard. I was just hoping that this was the distraction we needed for the others to exit his room. When we came up for air, I saw Alex closing the door. *Shit.* I tugged on the top of Nolan's jeans. He took that as a sign that I wanted more and gently pushed me against the wall, lifting my legs and urging me to wrap my legs around his waist. *I didn't want this. I didn't want to go this far.*

"Ahem." It was so good to hear Alex's voice.

Thank God. Nolan stopped kissing me. He slowly released me, and I slid back down.

"Lola, I thought that was you. I'm glad I ran into you. I know this is bad timing, but did you see the e-mail from our boss? He wants our report as soon as possible. I hate to bother you so late, but you have the most recent version of the PowerPoint."

"Yes, of course. I'll send it right now." I turned to Nolan, "I'm sorry about this. Thank you again for dinner. Work, it never ends even when you're in paradise," I said with my hands in the air. I started to walk away from Nolan. Alex followed me. "Oh, we were going to make that change in one of the figures. Do you have that information?" I added, tugging on Alex's sleeve to walk faster. Once inside the elevator, I took several deep breaths. "God, I wasn't sure how I was going to get out of that."

"It certainly didn't look like you wanted to end your night just yet," Alex replied, staring at the buttons on the elevator.

I took another deep breath. "I don't get you at all," I said, shaking my head at him. "Did you get anything from his laptop?"

"Yes, it took a while, but Beck finally hacked into his laptop. Amanda left some clothes in your room for you to change into. Meet us in the lobby in ten minutes. We're leaving tonight." Alex was definitely agitated.

"Fine," I said, leaving him in the elevator. I walked over to my room without looking back. I was too tired to figure out why he was in such a bad mood. I looked at my watch. It was almost two a.m.

I swiped my key card, and the door opened too easily. I lost my balance just as someone pulled me inside the room. Alarmed, I tried to regain my balance as quickly as possible.

"What took you so long? I missed you." The stranger whispered in my ear.

"Nolan," I whispered back, trying to get away from him. He held me tighter and nudged me to walk ahead of him. He flipped the lights on. "Now, tell me who you are and who you work for."

"I don't know what you're talking about."

He pulled a gun from his back and aimed it at me. "You were a better liar during dinner," he interjected, cocking the gun.

I took a few steps away from him. "What gave me away?"

"I have to admit you had me fooled. But you're not the type of girl to kiss on the first date."

Using air quotes, I replied, "The whole 'wrap my legs around you' bit was too much?"

He began to laugh. I knew I had a moment in which he would be absorbed in his laughter. I went for a punch in his stomach, but it didn't faze him at all. "God, you're funny." He seemed so amused at my futile attempt.

"That didn't hurt at all?"

"Not a bit." He continued to chuckle.

"I had to try. How about this?" I kicked him in the balls. He doubled over and dropped his gun. I ran into him, using my shoulders to knock him down. Then I ran for the door. He grabbed my ankles and I went facedown on the floor. *Damn, not again!* I gave a small cry from the pain I felt when I hit the floor. I quickly turned around to kick him off, but he was on top of me before I could position my leg. His hands quickly found their way around my neck. I forced my knee into his groin as hard as I could.

He groaned, "You bitch!" I used that moment to gasp for air. I tried to pry his fingers off my neck, but he just tightened his grip even more. I was blacking out. My lids were fluttering on their own. Images of women that he had conned flashed into my head. Some of them pleading with him as they finally realized their predicament. I didn't want to, but I was desperate as well. I could barely get the words out, "Please, stop." He let go of his grip around my neck, but he still had me pinned down. "You don't have to do this. You can stop and just walk away." I blurted out, coughing between words.

"So you know what I do?" I forced my head to nod. "What makes you think I wouldn't sell you?"

"You wouldn't."

"Don't be so naive. I would get top dollar for someone like you."

"I'm just a research assistant for a commercial real estate company. I really wouldn't be that profitable."

"Is that what this is all about? My business deal with the English guy?"

"What English guy?" He gripped my neck tighter again. "Please, you're hurting me." For a brief moment, we made eye contact, and I could feel his hands loosening. I couldn't keep my eyes from closing. I suddenly felt the weight of his body being yanked off of me. His hands were no longer around my neck, and I forced my eyes to open. Alex was hitting him. At first, Nolan fought back, and then I heard his neck snap. Nolan was dead.

I still couldn't get my breath back. I sat up coughing and chocking. "Breathe, Lyla. Try to make yourself calm down. Now is not a good time to have a panic attack." *You think?!* Alex took both my hands. "Now, focus on me. At the count of three, we'll take a short but deep breath." I nodded in reply. "Ready, one, two, three, breathe." I did what he told me to do.

The door opened again and Riley, Lupe, and Amanda walked in. "You guys okay?" Riley asked with a worried expression on his face.

"She's fine. We'll need a cleaning crew to dispose of the body." Alex responded.

"I'm on it," Lupe replied, pulling out her cell phone, but not before looking me in the eyes. I nodded in her direction. "Amanda, see if you can get his fingerprints, his real ones," I heard Lupe say. Amanda's suitcase clicked open.

Riley leaned in to check the marks on my neck. "Are you okay?" Anger flashed on his face.

"Yeah," I managed to say.

"Did he say anything to you?" Riley asked.

"He didn't know me. He asked who I was and who I worked for."

"Good, now let's get you out of here."

Alex and Riley helped me stand up. As soon as my feet touched the ground, my legs gave in. They placed me on the bed so I could sit down. "Riley, go get the car and I'll help her down." Riley nodded and left the room. "You ladies got it from here?" Alex asked.

"Yup, the cleaning crew will be here in five minutes," Lupe replied.

"You forget where I started from, darling," Amanda said, putting her gloves on.

"I can't carry you because that would look suspicious. Lean on me and I'll do the rest."

"I just need some water." In a flash, he was back at my side with a glass of water. Slowly, I drank the water. It hurt to swallow. I placed the glass on the bed stand.

"I'll take that, sweetie," Amanda said, taking the empty glass away. "We can't leave any prints behind."

"I think I can stand now." Alex helped me to my feet, and this time my knees held my weight.

My memories of the rest of the night were hazy. I was in the backseat of the car, and Riley was driving. Alex kept turning around to check on me. Then we got to the plane, and I was relieved to see Beck. I lay down next to him, and Alex put a blanket over me. The noise from his typing on his keyboard made me feel safe. I closed my eyes and fell asleep. Images of the time I'd spent with Nolan kept resurfacing in my dream.

chapter

TWENTY SEVEN

Alex

In the days following our return from Hawaii, I continue to make decisions regarding Lyla on a whim. Beck was able to obtain a list of more warehouse sites from Nolan's computer. I drove Lyla to the sites in no particular order. We visited most of the locations, and nothing out of the ordinary happened. She didn't feel any presence. Maybe it was a good sign. The bastard had been quiet for a while—there were no new killings.

Then one night she had another dream, and I woke up feeling an overwhelming sense of anxiousness from her. I rushed to her room. She had just woken up from her dream. I tried to hold her hand, but she pulled away. She closed her eyes and recounted her dream. She described another killing. She was willing to remember, and was very descriptive about the victim and the surroundings she saw in her dreams. The only thing she couldn't see was the killer's face.

I continued her training, believing that the best chance she had to survive whatever harm was waiting for her was to be able to defend herself. She was already very good with the sword. I was actually impressed with her sword skills. All those summers she'd spent in Japan paid off. In her file, there was a picture of her playing with a young boy, sparring with wooden sticks.

Sometimes Simon came to the house to train with her, and other days I drove her to the office for training. One day she was extremely quiet on our drive home. In the house, she headed straight for her room. "Flora made you dinner," I called out.

"Thank you, I'm not hungry."

I followed her. "You haven't said one word to me since we left Hawaii. What is it? Are you mad at me?" I couldn't stand Lyla's silent treatment anymore. "Just tell me so I can fix it." *Great, more silence.*

"You can't fix it." She started to walk up the stairs quickly. I shouldn't have installed the banister.

"Give me a chance." I took a few steps to catch up to her. "Is this about your mom? I can help you look for her."

"No, we don't ever need to talk about her." She turned around and stared straight at me. "He's dead. You can't fix it."

"Nolan?"

"Yes. He wasn't all that bad."

"He sold women and children for a living. Nolan didn't just supply the killer with convenient locations; he supplied him with the girls."

"I saw his eyes. He was going to let me go."

"Not this shit again." I let go of her hand.

"What gives you the right to kill people? Are you and I above the Ten Commandments? Because I'm pretty sure one of them is about not killing your fellow human beings. Do they not apply to us because we have these gift?"

Lyla barraged me with questions I couldn't answer. After I saw my mother killed trying to protect me, I didn't ask these types of questions anymore. Her words stung me. "I'm going to protect you no matter what."

"Can't you do it without hurting people?"

"Yes, I'll politely ask them to stop trying to kill you," I said, walking downstairs.

"Don't make fun of me."

"I'm not one of your groupies. I'm not head over heels in love with you and willing to do everything you ask." I was surprised by my answer.

"Leave my friends out this. You don't know anything about our friendship."

"Don't play stupid if you think these guys don't like you and you're not just stringing them along. Someone's bound to get hurt."

She slapped me. I'm not sure how I didn't notice her get close enough to slap me, but she did. We stood facing each other for a long time. I didn't have to use my abilities to sense that she was mad. I returned her glare. Ironically, all I wanted to do was kiss her, even though she had just slapped me.

Lyla broke the silence. "Of course they like me. They wouldn't be friends with me if they didn't like me, just the way I am. And I love them, but I'm not in love with them." She took a step away from me. "They love me, but they're not in love with me. There's a big difference, and we all know that." In a very small voice, she said, "We're family. I would do anything for them." Her voice rose, "And for the record, I would never use them or string them along. So stop thinking you know me because of some file you read about me. I will do you the same favor and not presume to think I know you either." We studied each other intently.

"I have no idea what you're talking about." I was confused, and my face still stung.

"I know! Half the time you don't know what I'm talking about." I guess she remembered me saying that.

I folded my arms to my chest. "Explain to me this love and being in love," I asked, mocking her tone.

"You love your brother and you love your father, but you are not in love with them. I love and care for my friends, but I am not in love with them. I will do anything for them, just about, and that is the difference. When someone is in love, he or she is willing to do anything without boundaries. When you're in love, you're willing to give more than what you get back, because you will always put that person first. Always! When you're in love, you risk everything, including your own happiness."

"Oh, please." I started walking down the stairs again.

"At least I'm open to idea of loving someone. You, you—" she stammered, trying not to blurt out what she was thinking.

"I am what, Lyla? What? Say it!" Lyla was striking a chord.

"You stopped living. It's like you're just waiting for an expiration date. It's worse than someone who is just passing through; you don't even want to be here."

We were both quiet, just holding each other's gaze, both unsure of what to say next. It was my turn to break the cold silence. "I'm going out for a while." I ran down the stairs and headed to the garage. I paused just before stepping through the doorway, "For God's sake, please don't do anything foolish." I left, not looking back.

chapter

TWENTY EIGHT

Lyla

I felt bad about what had just happened. I had never been comfortable with confrontation and couldn't recall ever getting into fights with anyone except with Matt. I realized that at least he never walked out on me, and our fights usually ended with me giving in and trying to make him feel better. *He never even gave me a chance*, I thought silently to myself.

I knew I wouldn't be able to sleep, so I didn't even try to go to bed. I decided to wait for Alex to return and apologize. After all, I was the one intruding in his home. I walked over to the living room. I looked over the remote controls neatly lying on the coffee table in order of their length, tallest to smallest. After an hour of channel surfing, I made myself more comfortable on the couch and closed my eyes, thinking about all the changes that had happened in my life. *It's all too much*, I thought. *Are all these things really happening to me? Or am I just having a really long nightmare?* With the last question in mind, I drifted off to sleep.

I woke up unsure how long I had been asleep on the couch and if Alex had come home yet. I stretched and screamed when I realized that I wasn't alone. There was a man sitting on the leather chair watching me.

"God, Alex, you scared me." Alex switched on the lamp next to him.

"Evans, you drool in your sleep." I quickly wiped my face, relieved not to find a pool of saliva in either corner of my mouth.

"No I don't. How would you know, you're sitting in the dark watching me. Stalker much?" I sat up.

"You're right, but you do snore."

I felt embarrassed; maybe I actually did snore. The training sessions were making me tired and exhausted. "Alex, I just wanted to apologize about what I said earlier. It was out of line. And for slapping you. I'm sorry." I kept my gaze on the floor.

"I know you didn't have a choice in staying here. And the last thing you want is to be stuck with me."

"That's where you're wrong. I have a choice. I am here because I choose not to die and you are my best bet for staying alive. So I choose to be here, stuck with you and your 'I can't be bothered' grumpy personality."

"I thought you were in the middle of apologizing."

"I was. I mean I am."

Alex stood up and walked over to the couch. He walked slowly; it looked like he was having a hard time supporting himself. I quickly got up and guided him to the couch. He groaned when I put his arm around my shoulder.

"Alex, are you okay?"

"Yes, I just need a minute."

I turned on the other lamp. "Are you hurt? I mean I can see that you're hurt and bleeding." With the light on, I could see that Alex was covered with cuts and bruises. I gasped when I noticed that his clothes were stained in blood.

"It's not my blood. I'm just banged up, that's all."

"I'll get you some water." I ran to kitchen and grabbed a bottle of water from the refrigerator.

"Here," I handed him the bottle of water. "Did you get into a bar fight?"

He laughed and placed a hand on his left ribs. "Ouch, it hurts to laugh." He let out a deep sigh, which caused him more pain. "I just need to take a shower." He took a few sips of the water and placed the bottle on the side table.

"I'll help you get upstairs."

"No, I think I can manage." Alex tried to get up but struggled to gain his balance. I quickly put his arms around my shoulders. Slowly, we went upstairs to his room.

When we finally arrived in his room, he winced when I grabbed the hand that was resting on my shoulder to steer him toward the bed. "I'm so sorry," I said, taking a close look at his knuckles. "They're pretty cut up. It looks like you were in a boxing match without gloves."

"I went a few rounds."

"Where did you go?"

"A warehouse near LAX. We finally stopped him before he could hurt another girl, but he escaped. Sorry," he said softly.

"You stopped him?" I asked.

"I knew exactly where to find him. Thanks to your dream. If I didn't, I would have been too late. He got away." I could see a look of disappointment on his face.

"The girl, is she okay?"

"She's in the hospital, but she's fine. A little scared, but her parents are with her."

"I should call Dr. Jenskee. You don't look so good."

"It's really not that bad. I look worse than I feel."

"I'll go turn the shower on." I walked to the bathroom. "I put the water temperature on warm to help ease your muscles. It looks like you have a few bruises." I walked back into the room and stopped when I realized that Alex was having a hard time trying to lift his shirt off with one hand. "Let me help you." I turned my head so I wouldn't be tempted to check him out. "There you go. Where do you keep your medicine supply in your house?" He winced again. "Did I hurt you?"

In shallow breaths, he replied, "Stop calling it my house. You live here too. In the kitchen."

I nodded and walked toward the door. I wasn't sure what he meant but decided not to ask right now. When I turned around, he was trying to unbutton his jeans with his good hand, but he wasn't having any luck. "Shit," he cursed to himself.

"Do you need help?"

He sighed, which made him wince in pain. "If you wouldn't mind...?"

I unbuttoned his jeans and became nervous when I realized I had to pull his zipper down. He quickly placed his hand on top of mine. "I think I can get it from here, thank you."

"Okay." I helped him with his shoes and socks. I looked up and realized that a dark bruise was beginning to form around his ribs. "Oh my God, Alex. You're really hurt. Maybe we should go to the hospital."

"No, I'm fine." I poked him around his ribs area. He gasped in pain.

"What did you do that for?"

"You're not fine."

"Alright, call Dr. Jenskee and ask him to come. I'll take a shower. I can't stand the filth that's on me right now." I helped Alex walk to the bathroom. He said thank you and closed the bathroom door.

Realizing that I didn't have Dr. Jenskee's phone number, I called Lupe. "Hey, girl." I was surprised to find her wide awake and she answered just after one ring. I apologized for calling so late and explained that I needed Dr. Jenskee's number.

"For Alex? Yeah, I heard he took on like a dozen men and got a pretty bad beating but refused to go to the hospital. He kept mumbling something about needing to get home and back to you."

"He's so stubborn. I was fine."

"Don't be too hard on him. He kicked ass and he did save a little girl's life tonight."

"I know."

"He couldn't have done it without you. The setup was exactly how you described it. The warehouse was huge; we would have spent most of the night trying to find our way around. Good job—and your man looked pretty heroic saving that girl."

"My man?"

"We'll talk later. I already sent Dr. Jenskee a text to head over. He should be there soon." I heard Lupe yawn. "Night, girl. Call me if you need anything else."

"Night, Lupe. Thanks." I had been wondering if she ever got tired. Apparently she did.

Not sure what else to do, I sifted through Alex's walk-in closet and found some pajamas and a white t-shirt. I placed his clothes on his bed. I heard the shower turn off and left his room to give him some privacy. Out in the hallway, my phone rang. It was Dr. Jenskee, giving me some instructions on what to do until he arrived.

I softly knocked on Alex's door before entering. "Don't put your shirt on yet. Dr. Jenskee told me to put on some of this ointment I found in your medicine supply."

"Lyla, I gotta lie down. I'm exhausted."

"Fine, I won't take long, and Dr. Jenskee is on his way." I paused and smiled. "You *do* know my first name."

He lay down in bed, and I noticed that he was staring at my face.

"Stop looking at me, you're making me feel awkward."

"You're killing me," he said aloud.

"I haven't even put the medicine on you yet."

I followed his gaze down to my body. The white cotton slip I was wearing was revealing too much, and it didn't help that I was standing in front of his lamp.

"Seriously?" I threw the bottle of ointment at him.

"Ouch," Alex laughed. I went to my room to get my robe. I walked back to his room and grabbed the ointment.

"I'm sorry, that wasn't very gentlemanly of me."

"No, it wasn't." I could feel my cheeks burning. I hoped he couldn't see that I was blushing.

"Does it hurt?" I asked. "This bruise looks like the shape of a lead pipe. Did someone hit you with a lead pipe?" Alex nodded. "If this is what you look like, I'd hate to see what the other guy looks like."

"He's walking around with a matching bruise on his face."

"Works for me," I replied, giving him a smile. He smiled back. *What I would do to wake up to that smile every morning.* The doorbell rang before I could continue my thoughts. Alex tucked a strand of hair that had fallen on my face behind my ear.

"Thank you." He continued to gaze at me.

"Should I get that? I mean, can I open the door? I'll look through the peephole first."

"We don't have a peephole." He reached over to the phone on his nightstand and pressed a button. Dr. Jenskee's face came on the screen. He pressed another button and told Dr. Jenskee that I was coming down.

I turned to leave the room. Alex reached for my hand and I turned back to face him. He pulled my robe tighter, "I tried really hard not to look, but I might have peeked a little." He smiled, his dimples were beaming, and he had a guilty look. *Alex, you take my breath away.* I had never realized what that saying meant until that moment.

I tossed a pillow on his face and walked out of the room. I led Dr. Jenskee back to Alex's room. He had fallen asleep in the few minutes since I left him. Dr. Jenskee poked around his ribs, and Alex woke up with a cry of pain. I stood by the wall to give the doctor space to work. I couldn't help myself—I sneaked a few peeks at Alex's bare chest and abs.

"You might have broken a rib or two," Dr. Jenskee announced. "I can't tell how bad it is without X-rays. We should get you to the hospital."

Firmly, Alex said, "No."

"All right, I understand. Get some rest and then come to my office in the morning," the doctor said, looking at his watch.

Dr. Jenskee reached into his bag and pulled out a vial of clear liquid and a syringe. "In the meantime, I'll give you something to help with the pain and bandage you up." Alex protested but the doctor went ahead and injected him. "Lyla, you did a good job of taking care of his minor wounds. Those should heal well."

"Thank you for coming. I'll walk you to the door." We went downstairs. I saw him out and closed the door behind him. I heard a click and assumed the door had automatically locked on its own.

I came back to Alex's room to check on him one more time. He was already asleep. I placed a glass of water on his bed stand and pulled his covers a little higher. I couldn't help myself. I placed my hand on his face and left it there a brief moment. I turned off the light and turned to go. I was surprised when Alex reached for the hem of my robe. In a whisper, he said, "Thank you."

"It's the least I can do, you know, for saving my life a few times. Good night, Alex." He still didn't let go, "Stay, please. Just until I fall asleep."

I reached for his hand and sat on the floor next to his bed. I sat there, content to hold his hand and to listen to him breathe.

chapter

TWENTY NINE

Alex

When I woke up, Lyla wasn't in the room. Flashes of last night quickly flooded my head. I reached for a pillow to cover my face. I groaned at the thought of all the embarrassing things I had just committed. *Stay until I fall asleep? When did I get so lame?*

I dressed and headed downstairs. I heard movements in the kitchen. I wondered who it was, since Flora had the day off. Lyla was standing by the stove. She looked up. "Hope you like French toast."

"Love it. Need any help?" I poured myself a glass of orange juice.

"No, I'm almost done. I just made some coffee." She pointed her spatula over to the coffee maker.

"I don't drink coffee."

She paused and looked at me. "Huh."

"What?" I pulled out one of the stools and slowly sat down. My ribs hurt even when I took a breath, and sitting on the stool took a toll on me.

"I've been living here for a while, and I never knew that." She placed a plate of French toast in front of me. "In fact, we've never even eaten together in your house."

"Let's do something about that," I said and patted the stool next to me.

"What smells so good?" Riley walked in and walked straight to Lyla. Standing behind Lyla's back, he looked over her shoulders. "She's beautiful and she can cook. Let's get married."

"Its French toast; I'd hardly call it cooking." Lyla gently slapped Riley's hand as he tried to grab a piece from the pan. "It's not ready yet."

Riley walked over to the other side of the kitchen island and tried to steal a piece from my plate. I smacked his hand away. "She made these for me."

"Bloody hell, what does a man have to do to get a piece of French toast around here?"

"Drive Alex to see Dr. Jenskee." Lupe walked in just in time to answer Riley's question. Lupe sat down on the stool next to me. I had to stop myself from frowning. Lyla sprinkled some powdered sugar and placed a plate in front of Lupe.

"Hey, I got here first!" Riley protested.

"Sorry, I ran out of bread."

"What?"

"Oh, come on, I'll share." Lupe handed Riley a fork.

"Finally, some compassion." Riley poured syrup and stuffed a mouthful of toast in his mouth. "Thanks, love." He gave Lupe a kiss while he was still chewing.

"Dios mio, that's gross, Riley. You've got syrup all over your lips." Lupe got up and washed off her cheeks.

"You ready, girl? We gotta go dress shopping."

"Dress shopping for what?" Lyla sipped her coffee.

"For the gala." Lupe turned to me. "You didn't tell her?"

I swallowed my food and mumbled, "I thought you were going to tell her."

"Same gala that your grandmother was talking about?" Lyla asked as she put her coffee cup down.

"Think of it as your coming out party," Riley chimed in, taking a big bite of toast. "Damn, this is good."

"My what?"

"Anyone who has 'the gift' comes to this event," Lupe made air quotes around the word *gift*.

"It's mostly political, new alliances are made and old ones are renewed," I added between bites.

"Or not." Riley took a gulp of my orange juice.

"That was my juice."

"So petty. The French toast is yours, the juice is yours, Lyla is yours." The room became still and silent. We could hear the birds chirping outside. I could feel my face getting hotter. Riley spoke again. "I was saying, remember the gala in 2008, Father lost his alliance with the Japanese? That was a bad year for us. You should have seen Father's face. He looked so heartbroken. This year, I heard our Venezuelan relationship is showing signs of weakness." I concentrated on chewing my food, unable to say anything to alleviate the awkward silence that continued to follow Riley's statement.

"Let's get you a dress." *Thank you, Lupe.*

"Okay, let me just grab a sweater. I'll be right back."

As soon as Lyla was upstairs, I punched Riley in the arm. "What's wrong with you?" It was worth it, even though I felt a shot of pain from my ribs.

"Touchy," Riley said as he rubbed his shoulders.

"Seriously, the two of you are only cool from afar, very far." Lupe started gathering her things.

"Is it just the two of you?" I asked Lupe.

"Would you let us go if it was just the two of us?"

"No."

"I didn't think so."

"Simon is coming with us, and we'll meet you at the office when we're done."

Lyla descended the stairs. "Ready," she announced. I opened the garage door for them, and they walked out to the car where Simon was waiting.

Riley drove me to the office. I groaned in pain every time the car hit a bump, hump, or pothole from my house to the office. I think he was driving over them on purpose.

Dr. Jenskee took some X-rays and gave me another shot. He said my ribs should heal fine. It would just take time. I was glad that we heal at a faster rate. I was struggling to put my shirt back on when Lyla tapped on the door and popped her head in.

"Hi; what did the doctor say?"

"He said I'll live."

"Let me help." She walked in and took the shirt from my hand.

"Done shopping?"

"Yup, forgot I already had a dress. Hands." I put my hands up. "Just had to go home and get it." She gently pulled my shirt down over my chest.

"There you go." For a moment, she held my gaze. I smiled. She placed her hand on my face. "Stop looking at me. I swear you have the ugliest smile, and those dimples. Scary."

"Do I scare you, Lyla?" I placed my hand on the small of her back and gently pulled her closer to me.

"Yes, what's with calling me by my first name all of a sudden... and why are you always looking at me lately?" She gently put my hand down away from her.

"Should I look somewhere else?" I looked down at her chest. She followed my gaze.

"Seriously, I expect that from Riley but not from you." She tilted my head up. I held her gaze steady. Her shirt had fallen to one side of her shoulder and I kissed her bare shoulder. I heard her let out a small sigh. She blinked and quickly tried to walk away, but she tripped on one of the pedals that were attached to the bed. I caught her in my arms and didn't hesitate. I kissed her.

chapter

THIRTY

Lyla

"Did you just kiss me?" I asked, unable to think reasonably.

Alex nodded. "And you kissed me back," he answered, with a smile that showed off his deep dimples.

"What happened to you last night? Did you get a concussion?"

He laughed.

"No, I just decided to be honest with my feelings. I finally have something to be scared about."

"What?"

"You're right, I've been living my life or not living my life. You finally gave me something to live for. Do you understand what I'm trying to say to you?" Alex asked.

"I don't understand half the things you tell me," I said. I flashed him a sheepish smile. We held each other's gaze. He leaned in, and I thought he was about to kiss me again. I would have let him.

The door opened, and a woman came in, a very gorgeous and sexy woman. "Alejandro, baby!" She ran to Alex. "Are you hurt, baby?" I automatically stepped back.

"Eva, what are you doing here?" I had never seen Alex look so surprised. He immediately jumped down from the bed. He winced in pain. *Good, I hope that hurt a lot.*

"Where does it hurt?" My eyes widened as I watched her kiss Alex on the forehead, the side of his face, and his hands. Alex tried to stop her, but she didn't pay him any attention and kept on kissing him. I was stunned, and all I could think of was, *Abercrombie model gets reunited with Victoria Secret model.*

"Eva, stop, I'm okay." He held the woman at bay.

I was walking out of the room when Riley walked in. He smiled at me but addressed the woman who was busy kissing Alex. "Eva, I see you found Alex."

"How could you let anyone hurt him?" Eva gave Riley an accusing look.

"You know how stubborn Alex can be. Eva, I would like you to meet Lyla." I was still inching away toward the door when I heard my name. I froze and looked back at Eva, who was now holding onto Alex's arm. Eva gave me a polite smile and I shook hands with her. Alex was quiet and stared at his shoes. *That's right, Alex, stare at the ground again.* "Nice to meet you," I said as politely as possible.

"Eva is from Venezuela. Her father runs the Venezuelan Organization." Riley turned to me with a naughty smile.

"Very nice to meet you, too." She greeted me in her sexy Latin accent. Then she immediately turned her attention back to Alex. "Alejandro, baby, let's go home and I will take care of you."

Alex pushed her away. "Eva, I'm sorry, I need to take Lyla home."

"Actually, Brother, Father said I should take care of Lyla until you recuperate."

"No, I'm fine."

As quickly as possible, I walked over to Alex and hit him dead center on his bruised ribs. He doubled over and let out a groan. "I wouldn't want you strain yourself. I think you need to let Eva take care of you."

"I like her." Eva flashed me a smile.

"Yeah, Father wants you to take it easy and maybe focus on rebuilding some international relationships." Riley winked at Alex. I turned to leave the room.

"Lyla, wait, can I talk to you first?" Alex called out after me.

I gave him big smile. "Of course, we can talk later. But right now, let Eva take care of you." I walked out. In a few seconds, Riley was behind me. He joined me in the elevator. Once the door closed, he reached over me to press the button. "You're sexy when you're jealous."

I didn't say anything because I knew he was baiting me. "She has the same gift as me, she can persuade people." A moment later, he added, "Better than me, I'm afraid."

"She has more assets to persuade with." We both laughed. Once we were in the car, I asked, "Where are we going?"

"Anywhere you want." I checked my watch.

"Do you like bowling?"

"Not sure. Will I?" He gave me a questioning look.

"Big balls, pins, and chicken wings, what's not to like?"

I gave Riley directions to the bowling alley I knew the boys would be at. Lance's grandmother made him join her bowling league. Of course, Lance didn't want to go alone and persuaded Beck and David to join as well. Every third Thursday of the month at three p.m., the boys bowled with a bunch of retired Asian men and women. It was the only time Lance's grandmother was able to see him. Lance's grandfather had disowned his parents, including Lance, when his father was incarcerated for life.

I smiled when I saw Lance, Beck, and David at their usual lane. They were wearing their tacky bowling shirts. "Hey, look who decided to grace us with her presence!" Lance was sarcastic, a dead giveaway that he was mad at me.

I gave him a hug first. "Sorry; work has been hectic."

"We heard. They got you flying to Hawaii, huh?" I gave Beck a look.

"Yeah, just for a quick meeting. I didn't even get to go to the beach." I gave Beck a high five and David a quick hug. Beck and Riley greeted each other.

"Guys, this is Riley. Alex's brother." Lance and David greeted him as well. "He has never played before, so take it easy on him."

"Come join the winning team," Lance said loud enough for opposing team to hear as he pointed at himself and the rest of us.

"Are we going to play or what? You know we ain't getting any younger," a member of the opposing team yelled back, and their group laughed.

"The old man got jokes!" Lance shouted back.

"I probably get more action too." We all laughed. We played a few games. Riley almost slipped a few times as he first tried to bowl. He got along well with the boys. By the time we started our second game, it felt like we had known him for a long time. The older women flocked to him, and he talked to them with his English accent, which got them even more excited.

Beck's last strike saved us from losing. Even though we had been munching on nachos and chicken wings all afternoon, we decided to eat. During the meal, the boys swapped sports stories. "How long has it been since we last sat down for a meal together?" Beck asked. Lance gave me an accusing look. If he only knew how much I had missed them. How lonely I had been without them. I laughed at their jokes, but I couldn't shake a feeling I had that it was never going to be the same again. *Because I'm not the same.*

David leaned in closer to me, "Are you okay?"

"Yeah." I gave him a smile. "I just really miss you guys."

"We miss you too."

"Hey, Lyla," Lance called from the other side of the table. "I need to get to the club soon to open up, but since you're so busy now that you're a research analyst and all, I don't know when I'll see you again. Why don't we head to the club for a few drinks before it opens?"

"Drinks? The sun is still up."

"It's officially dusk," Beck pointed out. He pointed outside the window. The sun was quickly setting.

"Oh, sure, as long as the sun is going down; it would be bad if we were drinking in broad daylight." It wasn't hard to convince me; I didn't want to leave my friends yet either. Our drinks lasted several rounds. We found ourselves on the dance floor showing off our 80s and 90s dance moves. Riley was the best one out of all of us. I think he must have been really tipsy when he shared with us that as a young boy, his dream was to be in a boy band.

Lance came up to me while I was alone at the table. My feet hurt from dancing and I needed to take a break. He jokingly said, "First the boss and now the brother. I hope you know what you are doing?" He handed me another drink. I looked over to Riley who was dancing with a group of girls and David and Beck were at the bar.

"I am not doing anything. I mean it." I replied taking a sip of my drink.

"Okay, I believe you." Lance got up and gave me a kiss on my forehead.

I had a horrible feeling I wasn't going to see them for a while, and I cherished every moment of that day. I hugged them a little bit longer than usual when we finally parted. David whispered in my ear, "Is everything really okay with you?"

"I miss you. Take care of Beck and Lance." Before he could say anything, I turned to walk to Riley's car.

It was past midnight when we pulled into Alex's driveway. He was already at my door before I could unbuckle my seatbelt. He opened the door and leaned inside the car. "Do you have any idea what time it is?" Riley and I looked at each other.

"Late, so I won't be coming in for a nightcap." Riley turned the engine over.

"Why didn't you answer my calls?" Riley picked up his cell phone from the console while I searched for mine in my purse. Sure enough, 'missed call' was blaring back at me.

I got out of the car and skirted around Alex. "Sorry," was all I could say. I waved goodbye to Riley, and he quickly backed out of the driveway. I could feel Alex's heavy breathing behind me as I walked to the door.

Once inside, I turned to Alex and said, "Well, it's late so... good night," and headed upstairs.

"Wait, we need to talk." He grabbed my hand.

"I'm really tired, Alex." I took my hand back.

"You wouldn't be if you had come home earlier. I was beginning to think something happened. I almost dispatched a Search Team."

"I already said I was sorry. I really didn't mean to worry you."

"Where were you?"

"Just hanging out with my friends."

"I see."

"I'm going up to my room."

"Just give me a minute, please. I just want to explain about Eva." I hated hearing him say her name. "I don't want you to get the wrong idea."

"No need. I don't have any idea about you or Eva, right or wrong. I'm really tired." I started walking up the stairs. *How did it get so messy?* I was halfway up the stairs when I turned around, "Stop trying to read me."

"I wouldn't need to if you'd just talk to me."

"Good night, Alex." I walked into my room.

chapter

THIRTY ONE

Lyla

In the morning, Alex stopped by my room, but I pretended to be asleep. He walked in and walked out. I lay in bed and ended up falling asleep again. My dream last night had really disturbed me. Alex had rushed into my room, but I dismissed him, telling him that I was fine and couldn't remember anything from the dream.

I was so disturbed by the dream that I couldn't fall back to sleep for a long time. It was the same dream I've often had that always ended with a blade stuck in my gut. However, last night's version felt different, even though nothing different happened in my dream. The scenes were more complete and just felt final and more imminent.

Around lunch time, Flora brought me my meal. She found me sitting in the middle of the floor studying all the papers that I had posted on my wall. "It doesn't look like you were planning to go downstairs, so I brought the food up to you." She looked at me with concern.

"Thank you, Flora." I grabbed a sandwich. "Delicious." I covered my mouth.

"Here, drink this before you choke." She handed me a glass of juice.

"Flora, have you ever met Dr. Rogets?"

"Once or twice, but I didn't care for him."

"Why?" I asked too quickly. I didn't expect that to be Flora's answer.

"He reminds me of a man my grandmother used to talk about. She was a survivor, you know, Auschwitz camp."

"Dr. Mendel?"

"You've heard of this evil man?"

"In fifth grade, I read *Diary of Anne Frank,* and then I wanted to read everything I could about the holocaust."

"It was a horrible time."

"Why does Dr. Rogets remind you of Dr. Mendel, Flora?"

"Oh, let's see. He is a curious man. Too curious, maybe."

"I know what you mean."

"You need to get ready for the gala soon. No?"

"Yeah," I answered, with no enthusiasm. "Are you going?"

"Me?" She pointed to herself. "No, only people with gifts like yours go to the gala."

"Can I get out of it, you think?"

"You remind me of me when I was younger. I always begged my father to persuade my mother not to make me go to boring parties."

"Exactly," I said with my head down.

"But then you grow old like me and then there are no more parties to go to."

"Oh."

"I will draw you a bath." I spent another hour in the bathtub thinking and sorting things out. I just finished taking a bath when I heard a soft knock on my door.

"Come in," I called. Lupe walked in with my dress.

"I thought you might need this."

"Thank you." I took the dress from her and laid it out on the bed. "What about you? What did you decide to wear?"

She unzipped the other garment bag that she was holding. "I was hoping that you would ask." She pulled out a deep burgundy, sequined dress.

"Wow, that's beautiful."

"I was also hoping I could get dressed here. I have three brothers, one sister, and one bathroom."

"Of course, it will be fun dressing together." I was thankful for Lupe's company. She was helping me forget about my dream last night.

"Thanks, and thank you for letting me use your dress allowance."

"I'm glad it worked out." On our way to the stores, I had learned from Lupe that Alex's father sanctioned an unlimited budget for any dress I chose. I also found out that Lupe was planning to wear a bridesmaid's dress she wore to her cousin's wedding. I remembered a dress I had bought on an impulse. It was still hanging in my closet, never worn because I had never had an occasion to wear it. I told Lupe my plan; it took me a while to convince her to go along with it.

Lupe and I chatted as we put our makeup on. She talked about her brothers and sister and how happy she was to work for the company because it helped her to take care of her family. Her father worked as an airline mechanic, but with the economy, his job was unstable. Her mother was a nurse, but her arthritis had gotten worse and worse until she couldn't work anymore. "She died three years ago. I don't think she even realized that she had a gift." Lupe added in a solemn voice. I wasn't sure what to say, so I just nodded my head hoping she understood I knew how hard it was to lose a parent.

As far as she could tell, she was the only one of her siblings with the gift. When her mother couldn't work anymore, Lupe had stopped going to college to look for a full-time job. She was offered a job at the company. Like me, she was eventually told about her gifts.

"Although I think my youngest sister, Alicia, might have the gift as well." She plugged in her curling iron. "She's only seven, and the other day she asked me to buy this doll. She tried to describe it to me, but I had a hard time understanding her. And then, poof, I had a visual of a doll in my head."

She helped me curl my hair, and I helped her straighten hers. "We always want what we don't have," I commented. Lupe's hair was naturally curly and my hair was straight.

Two hours later, we were done. I gave myself one last look in the mirror. "That dress is perfect for you," Lupe said, looking at my reflection in the mirror.

"Can you believe I found this dress on the sale rack? It was marked down after being marked down. I took one look at it and knew I couldn't leave it behind, just hanging there unwanted. It was begging me to take it home."

"Are you serious? I thought it was some fancy couture dress. It's beautiful."

"It's not too much pink?" The dress was a strapless pink ball gown that fell short of an inch above my knees. I would normally not wear something so pink and princessish, but the designer had added a black leather corset, and it just blended so effortlessly.

"It's perfect." Lupe twirled me around.

"And you, Miss Martinez, are beautiful."

On cue, Lupe's cell phone beeped. She picked it up. "We're ready. We'll be right down." She put the cell phone back in her evening purse. "Simon is downstairs. He's going to drive us. Alex had to pick up Eva. He'll meet you there."

"Okay."

"There's nothing serious going on between Alex and Eva. I mean, the girl tries, but Alex would never—"

I cut her off. "Alex is a guy, and Eva looks like a Victoria Secret model. Even Leonardo DiCaprio can't keep his hands off them."

"Okay, but you can't deny that Alex has fallen hard for you."

"I don't know. I just want my old life back."

"I know what you mean. I still wish I could just finish college, you know."

"I do. I really do." We gave each other a hug. "All right, let's go before we start crying. I'm pretty sure I didn't use waterproof mascara."

Flora was waiting for us downstairs with Simon. She was carrying a Polaroid camera. She gasped when we came down. "Both of you look so beautiful. I have to take pictures."

"Flora, can you still buy Polaroid film?" I asked her.

"Don't make fun of me. I want my pictures as soon as possible. If you have faced death like I have, you don't want to wait for such things. Now come on, you two stand over there." We did, and Flora took several pictures. We giggled as we looked at the pictures that automatically came out of the camera.

"Can I take one?" I asked her.

"Of course. See, convenient, right?" I took a picture of Lupe and myself smiling at each other. I placed it in my clutch.

When we got in the car, I turned to Lupe. "I'm nervous."

"Why?" She gave me a look of concern.

"I don't know. I just am." I gave her a smile. "It's probably because I've never been to a gala before."

"You'll be fine," she tried to reassure me. I lied. I knew my nerves had nothing to do with the gala.

An hour later, Simon pulled up in front of the hotel. Someone opened our door, and Lupe and I both got out of the car. When we walked into the lobby, I heard a whistle. "Ladies, your beauty has left me speechless." Riley looked very handsome in his tuxedo.

"Not so bad yourself." Lupe elbowed him in the stomach.

I looked around. A feeling of familiarity was growing inside of me. *I've seen this lobby before.* I closed my eyes and realized it was part of my dream last night. Suddenly I realized that someone was saying my name.

"Lyla?"

"What?"

"You okay?" Riley asked me.

"Yeah, sorry, I must have inhaled too much hairspray. It's making my head foggy." Riley and Lupe laughed.

"I asked if you wanted a drink, and it looks like you need one." Riley looked past my shoulder. I turned around in time to see Alex and Eva walking in. Alex looked stunning in his tuxedo, and Eva was beautiful, her arm wrapped around his.

Alex quickly dropped her arm when he saw us. Riley grabbed two glasses of champagne from a passing waiter and gave them to Lupe and me. "No, thank you," I said. I was already feeling funny, and I didn't think champagne would help.

Alex and Eva walked over to us. "Hello, everyone," Eva greeted us. She was charming. You couldn't deny that.

"Lyla, you look beautiful." Alex tried to make eye contact with me but I kept my eyes lowered.

"Thank you; you both look stunning."

"Yes, what a lovely dress. Who are you wearing?" Eva asked with sincerity in her voice. It was hard not to like her.

"Uh…" I didn't really want to share with her that I had found my dress on the sales rack.

Alex saved me. "Lupe, forgive me. You look lovely as well."

"Thank you. I was starting to feel like chopped liver." We all laughed politely.

"Chopped liver has nothing on you," Riley chimed in. "We should head inside the ballroom. I'm sure Father must be wondering where we are." We headed toward the massive double doors.

I lagged behind the group and somehow Alex managed to wind up beside me. "We need to talk, Lyla." He grabbed my hand to lead me in a different direction. I tried to shake my hand free, but he held it firmly.

"Nico, Lyla, there you are." It was Alex's grandmother. She stepped in front of us, gave each of us a hug, and kissed our cheeks.

"You look so beautiful," I told her.

"Nights like these are not for old ladies like me, but for beautiful young woman like you." She took a step back to get a better look at me. "You remind me so much of Delilah." I quickly grabbed her hand.

"You knew my mother?"

"Why, yes, she and Alex's father were childhood friends." I wanted to ask more questions, but an announcement came requesting that we all take our seats. "Please, I never knew my mother. Can you tell me about her?"

"I will gladly answer all your questions." She patted my hand. "Come, you and Nico are sitting next to me at my table." I followed her. Alex held the chair for his grandmother and I sat down next to her before he could pull my chair out for me. Marsha sat next to me. I politely greeted Marsha, and she introduced me to her husband, who sat next to her. Alex took the seat on the other side of his grandmother. Once we were seated, I continued to ask her my questions. "When was the last time you saw my mother?"

With a frown, Rose answered, "I'm sorry. I don't remember the last time I saw her. I didn't even know she was pregnant with you." The emcee came on stage. I had to wait to ask my questions until he stopped talking. That's when I realized that Eva was sitting next to Alex and an older gentleman was sitting next to her. *That must be her father.* Martin was sitting next to the older man.

Halfway through pushing my dinner around, I couldn't be patient anymore. I leaned toward Alex's grandmother and said, "I'm sorry. I know it's terribly rude of me but I have to ask, is my mother still alive?"

Alex's grandmother looked over at Martin. He nodded. She turned back to me. "I really don't know, dear." She patted my hand again.

"I guess it would also be pointless for me to ask if you know why she would just abandon me?"

She looked at me; I think she was trying to read me. "I know that she is not the kind of woman who would leave her child if she didn't have a very good reason." She held my chin and stroked my face. I excused myself from the table and headed out into the lobby. I heard Alex call my name.

"Alex, I'm sorry. I stopped asking about my mother a long time ago. I don't know why I asked those silly questions. I guess I just wanted to know before it all ends. Please apologize to your grandmother."

"Where are you going?"

"Home—no, sorry." I stopped myself. "Back to your house, and I promise not to do anything foolish."

"I'll go with you."

"No."

"I'll take you home."

"Simon can take me. You came here with someone else, and you need to go home with the same person. Good night."

I walked out of the lobby and saw Simon standing by the car. I ran to the car and didn't wait for him to open the door. "Get me out of here, Simon." Ten minutes later, Simon pulled off the freeway.

"Where are we going?"

Simon pushed a button and locked all the doors. "I'm really sorry about this."

"Simon, what are you doing?" He pulled out a white cloth and placed it over my mouth. I tried to struggle, but within a few seconds my eyelids became heavy and I lost control of my arms and legs. "Simon, please don't do this."

"I'm sorry, Lyla."

chapter

THIRTY TWO

Lyla

I woke up on a bed in a room that I didn't recognize. I got up, feeling hazy and groggy. My shoes and clutch were on the floor next to the bed. As soon as my legs could hold my weight, I ran to the window and checked outside. I was on the first floor with a view of a courtyard. There was a tree—*the cherry tree in my dreams*. I tried to open the windows, but none would budge. I ran to the door; it was locked. I threw a lamp at the window and it bounced back. *Dammit.*

I quickly turned when I heard the doorknob turn. Simon walked in. "Are you okay?"

"Simon, help me, please." I ran to Simon and pleaded with him.

He wouldn't look at me. "Please follow me."

"Fine." I pretended to walk toward the door. When I knew he was directly behind me, I turned to kick him. He anticipated my move and caught my foot.

"Lyla, please, I don't want to hurt you." He placed my foot down. Of course, he knew my moves. He had trained me. I followed him. He led me out into a hallway, and we walked to the end of the hall toward a set of double doors. He opened the door and waited for me to walk in first.

The room was a library. Three of the walls had floor-to-ceiling bookshelves filled with books that were carefully organized by color of the binding. A large desk was set in the middle of the room. The sun was shining, and it was too bright for me to see who was sitting behind the desk. I stepped forward.

"You don't look very surprised, Ms. Evans."

"Not really...creepy scientist with a lab in the basement. I don't know why I didn't figure it out sooner."

"Then I'm sure you know what will happen next."

"I'll die." I looked around the room.

"Unfortunately, yes. Don't take it personally, but your gifts are getting to be bothersome."

"I'm sorry you were inconvenienced."

"I was," Dr. Rogets smiled. His smile made him look even creepier. I felt my stomach flip. "Simon, bring the girl out."

"Didn't realize you were the fetching type." Simon did not answer me and continued to walk out of the room. I walked over to a narrow table with swords displayed on top. The hilt looked familiar. The door opened, and a little girl walked in with Simon's hand on her shoulder. Her eyes were swollen and tears were rolling down her cheeks.

I glared at Simon. "I guess you are the *fetch me* kind."

"Does she look familiar to you?" Dr. Rogets asked, getting up from his chair and walking over to the little girl. I shook my head.

He bent down to face the girl. "Hi, Alicia. Don't cry. I'm doing this for your own good." He wiped her tears away with the back of his hand. The girl tried to take a step back but couldn't go very far since Simon was still behind her. She looked very scared. I wanted to run to her.

"Interesting; so you didn't dream of her even though you are so close to her sister?" Rogets stood up and turned to me. "Oh, how I wish I could study you more. Your gifts fascinate me, but my calling is more important." Simon, take these two back to their rooms. Make sure everything is ready. We leave tonight. He patted the top of the girl's head.

Simon kept his hand on the girl's shoulder. "Don't try anything, Lyla, or I'll break the girl's neck." I had a feeling he was serious. I walked out of the library with Simon and the little girl behind me. I walked back to my room obediently. I heard the lock click behind me and pressed my ear to the door. I counted Simon's steps and heard a door open and close. Alicia was being kept down the hall from me.

I listened until I could no longer hear Simon's footsteps. I looked around the room for a weapon but found nothing I could use. I lifted my skirt and pulled out the pick set Riley had given me for my birthday. I had made it a habit to keep it on me at all times and tonight I had strapped it on my thigh. I picked the lock and listened again for any noise. When I was convinced that there wasn't anyone in the hallway, I grabbed the Polaroid picture from my clutch and quietly walked out of the room. I walked twenty steps in the direction I thought Simon and Alicia had walked.

I picked the lock, entered the room, and quickly closed the door behind me. The room was empty. It only took me a second to figure out where I would hide if I was Alicia and I was very scared. I walked over to the bed and laid down flat on the floor. "Alicia," I whispered, "my name is Lyla and Lupe is my friend." Alicia crawled farther away from me. I pushed the Polaroid picture underneath the bed. "See?" I placed the picture near her. She slowly picked it up.

"You know my sister."

"Yeah, she's a good friend of mine from work."

"Do you have gifts too?"

"Yes, I dreamed about you."

"You told that man you didn't know me."

"I lied, but I promise you, I won't lie to you."

"Promise?" I could barely hear her.

"I promise. Can you come out, please? We need to get out of here."

She began crawling out, and when she was halfway out, I pulled her the rest of the way and picked her up. "Alicia, Lupe told me that you have a gift as well. You can put images in people's heads." She nodded.

"Can you do it now? Can you put that man's face in your sister's head?"

"The creepy one?"

"Yeah, the creepy old one."

"I can't."

"Just try for me, please." She nodded and closed her eyes. I prayed to God that it would work. "Thank you, Alicia." I hugged her tight. "You have to promise to listen to me at all times and be as quiet as possible."

I had a decision to make, and I knew immediately what my answer was. I would protect this little girl. Even if it meant that I needed take the life of others. As soon as I had made my decision, I remembered the swords Rogets proudly displayed in his library.

I grabbed Alicia's hand and beckoned her to follow me. Quietly, we made our way to the back of the mansion, to the library. I was relieved to find it empty. I tried to let go of Alicia's hand., but she wouldn't let me. "It's okay. I won't let anything happen to you. Just promise me that you will do everything I ask you to do." She nodded in response and let go of my hand. I placed her hand on the back of my dress. This gave her a sense of security. At that moment, it was all I could do for her. I lifted each of the twin swords, surprised by their lightness.

I just had enough time to make a few slashes in the air when the door opened and Simon and half a dozen men stormed in. Alicia screamed. Firmly, I told her to hide underneath the desk. "Don't come out until I tell you to. Hurry!"

I didn't have time to look and see if Alicia had done what I told her. I knew one of the men was within reach of the sword, and reflexes made me turn around and swung my right sword at an angle toward his neck. The reality that I had just killed a man hit me when his blood splattered on my face. All those summers I had spent sparring with wooden sticks with my friend left us with bruises at the worst, but it had never ended with a man's life. I turned to face another man running toward me on my left. I took a step to meet him and, with a flick of my left wrist, I pointed the sword down through his left thigh. With the sword in my right hand, I stabbed him in the abdomen and he fell to the floor.

Somehow, I stopped the other four men. When I finally stopped to turn around, they were all on the floor dead. The scene reminded me of Quentin Tarantino's movie *Kill Bill*. In fact, it felt like I was watching a movie and not actually the person creating this horrific scene.

Only Simon was left. "Why, Simon?"

"Because my dad died as a security guard, not amounting to anything, and that's not going to happen to me. It took me five years before they even let me wear a suit. Rogets believed in me. I'm in charge here." He looked around at the dead bodies of the men he used to be in charge of.

"Rogets killed all those children. You can't really want to be a part of that."

"If you only try to understand him, you can join us and I won't have to hurt you."

"I don't want anything to do with Rogets. I want to stop him. You can help me. Please."

"Then you give me no choice."

"You always have a choice—" He never let me finish my sentence. He charged me, but I also knew his weakness from all the times we'd spent talking in the car. I jumped out of the way and landed on his knee. I heard it crack under my weight. "How's that football injury?" He cried in pain and went down on his good knee. I didn't hesitate, stabbing him at angle through his neck.

I wiped the blood that splattered on my face with a blanket that was carefully laid on the back of the brown leather couch, then I walked over to the desk where Alicia was hopefully hiding. Mr. Rogets had left his scarf on his seat. I used it to wipe the blood on each of the swords, holding both of them with my left hand. Relieved to find Alicia crouched in the corner underneath the desk, I pulled the chair out of the way and extended my right hand. "Alicia, come out, but I want you to close your eyes, okay? Promise me."

"My eyes are closed, Lyla." She grabbed my hand.

I carefully walked Alicia around the bodies. We were halfway down the hallway that led to the main door when I heard the shuffling of feet coming toward us. A group of men, twice as many as the group in the library, was fast approaching us. I gently shoved Alicia to the wall and let go of her hand. "Stay behind me."

I pulled one of the swords from behind me and threw it at the man leading the chase. I aimed straight for his throat. Just as I predicted, the sword went straight through the man's throat and, when his head pulled back, I saw that it also cut the man running directly behind him. This man was shorter, and the blade stuck him between his eyes. This caused enough distraction among the men chasing us. Just enough time for me to point at the door and whisper, "Alicia, you need to run as fast as you can toward those doors. Don't look back. Keep running."

"No, I can't." Alicia started crying.

"You need to." I shoved her toward the main door. "Run!"

I turned toward the rest of the men, who were now just a few feet away from me. I heard Alicia's footsteps and knew that she was running toward the door. Again, I went on autopilot. I didn't have a single thought but to stop these men. I had to give Alicia as much time as possible.

I was getting weary, but I was glad that the number of men had dwindled to half. I was ready to attack again when I heard a familiar click near my head, and then I felt a push on my head by what I presumed was a gun.

"You've been making a mess in my house, Lyla." Rogets whispered in my ear, with an edge to his tone. "Drop the sword before I lose my patience." I let the sword slide out of my hands; it made a noise as it fell on the marble floor.

"What are you standing there for? Find the little girl!" The men looked at each other and started to walk away from us and toward the door.

"Wait, stop!" I yelled. "What's the plan? A bunch of grown men chasing after a little girl in broad daylight: that's not conspicuous at all. What will your neighbors think?"

"Run, you idiots! Don't you see she's just trying to stall?" I turned around to face Rogets. His men started running. He kept the gun pointed at me. "You just can't get good help these days."

"These men don't look like your everyday street thugs."

Rogets smiled again. "Hiring the street thugs was just to keep the St. James boys busy."

"They know that you kill innocent children?"

"Of course, Lyla. They believe in my cause. I wish that you would too. We are very alike, you and I."

"I'm nothing like you."

"Now, now, let's not lie to ourselves. There are men, including Simon, who have lost their lives because of you."

"But I—"

"Shh, Lyla. At the end of the day, you killed these men."

"I did it to protect Alicia, to save her life."

"You don't need to convince me. In fact, you're preaching to the choir. I applaud your effort. Unfortunately, it ends here. How far do you think that little angel can go? My men will find her, and then she will have to die because I'm saving her."

"That doesn't even make any sense." He must have seen the confused look on my face.

"Don't you get it? It's my duty to ensure that these little innocent children go to heaven. When they grow up, well, you know what they turn out to be. They lie and steal—or worse." He paused and touched my cheek with the back of his hand. It gave me the chills. "Or worse, Lyla, they give in to temptation and become evil." I slapped his hand away. "It's my duty, you see, to ensure that doesn't happen."

"So you kill them to make sure they don't grow up to be bad?"

"I save them. I'm glad you finally understand. I'm just doing what I was destined to do. I save—"

"You're a psychopath." I didn't let him finish his sentence. I kicked the gun out of his hand and lunged toward the floor to grab the sword. He was too fast. He picked up the sword before I could reach it. He kicked me in my kneecap and I fell onto my back.

Out of the corner of my eye, I noticed the gun lying beside me. Still on the floor, I grabbed the gun and turned around. He was arched on top of me, holding the hilt of the sword with two hands, ready to plunge. I fired twice and he fell on the floor next to me. The gunpowder hit me on the face and I blinked.

When I opened my eyes, I saw the sword standing on its own, just like in my dream. I followed it down and went into shock when I realized that it was lodged in me. *Oh, so that's how it happens.* I swallowed a small pool of blood that had started to make me choke. I pulled the sword out of me.

Rogets's blood was quickly making a pool around his body. I didn't want to die near his body. I made myself get up, and a rush of blood spilled out of my abdomen as I pulled myself up. I walked a few steps toward a set of French doors. I was glad that they weren't locked. They opened onto a small courtyard. I struggled to walk over to the cherry tree in the middle of the courtyard. *If I had to choose a tree to die next to, it would be a tree full of cherry blossoms.* With difficulty, I finally reached the tree and slumped down as another gush of blood streamed out of my wound. I closed my eyes and prayed that Alicia got away. *Please, God, please save her.*

I was getting sleepy, and I wanted to give into my weariness. I tried to think. *Shouldn't I be fighting to stay alive? But if I die now, no one else will ever leave me behind.* It seemed like a good enough reason to let go, so I closed my eyes.

❦

"Lyla, Lyla, please wake up. She's over here!" I felt pressure on my wound. I wasn't sure how much time had passed. "Lyla, please hold on."

I opened my eyes and saw Alex's face. I was grateful that I could see him one last time, "A...Alicia?" I asked, coughing up blood.

"She's safe."

"Lyla, please just hang on. Please. I don't want to lose you."

"I'm tired, Alex. Let me sleep." The world went dark.

❦

"Hello, Lyla." I opened my eyes and realized I was in the hospital. I ached everywhere and my head was pounding.

"It's time go home." A man's voice whispered.

I recognized this man. "Yusuke?" I studied his face for a long time. He looked different—older and more handsome. I had not seen Yusuke since the last time I was in Japan before I went to college.

"I'm taking you home. Oji-san has been waiting for you." He began to take off the tubes that were attached to my hand and arm.

"Oji-san?" Yusuke nodded.

"I'm going home?"

"Yes," he whispered with a smile. I smiled back, taking his hand.

Epilogue

Alex

"What do you mean she's gone?" I lost it and grabbed the doctor by his collar. Riley stepped in and made me release my hold on the doctor. The doctor hastened to leave the room.

"She's gone, Alex," Riley said in a whisper.

"Kidnapped?" I should have never left her.

"She walked out on her own. I checked the security tapes. She left with a man," Riley explained.

"A man? One of her friends?"

"No, this man was Asian, maybe Japanese. Beck is working on his facial recognition as we speak. But—"

"But what?" I yelled back.

"She was holding his hand. There was no sign that she was being forced to leave with him." Riley stepped back from me.

Father walked in and placed a hand on my shoulders. "She is safer with them. She is where she is supposed to be."

"What are you talking about? This isn't a good time for your secrets, Father."

"She's with her family; they can protect her better than we can."

"No, she said she has no family. Her father died last year." I tried to reason with them.

"Let her go, for now." My father held me.

"How? When I don't even know where she is? I need to protect her...I..." I stopped, unable to complete the sentence in front of my father.

"You need to let her go because right now she needs to be with her family." My father looked at me with a steady gaze. He put a picture in my mind of Lyla when she was a little girl. She was with an old man. They were fishing. She called him Oji-san. She seemed happy. They were singing a song in Japanese.

"The man is her grandfather, leader of the Japanese Warrior Clan. Both Delilah and Lyla's father have gifts," my father said in a steady voice.

"Which makes Lyla full-blooded," Riley trailed of at the end and didn't finish his sentence. We were both realizing the impact of what Father was telling us.

"No one knows the extent of Lyla's abilities yet. That's why she needs to be with her family. They can help her and keep her safe."

"But I need her, Father. I'm in love with her," I said in a steady voice.

"Who isn't, little brother?" Riley and I stared at each other.

About the Author

Rhea Sanchez lives in Southern California with her husband, their two sons, and their dog. A perfect day for her is a day spent with her family, which consists of Joseph, Jaden and James, Lolo and Lola, JJ and Roselle, Brent and Reggie and her nieces and nephews: Raquel, Brandon, JR, Reese and Sophia. When she is not writing or teaching, she loves reading books and watching sitcoms and movies.

Rhea is currently working on her next two books, *Alex St. James* (the sequel to Lyla Evans) and *The Unfortunate Tale of Dev and Jess* (a completely new story). Her goal is to have both books completed by the end of the year. She hopes her family, friends, and readers will love the new books as much as they loved Lyla Evans.

www.ingramcontent.com/pod-product-compliance
Lightning Source LLC
Chambersburg PA
CBHW020412180626
46812CB00003B/939